Copyright © 2018 by Tansy Rayner Roberts

ISBN: 978-0-6483291-0-7 (ebook)

ISBN: 978-0-6483291-1-4 (print)

Cover art @2018 Kathleen Jennings

Cover typography & design @2018 Catherine Larsen

✿ Formatted with Vellum

CABARET OF MONSTERS

A CREATURE COURT NOVELLA

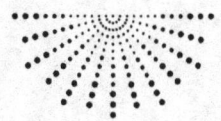

TANSY RAYNER ROBERTS

For all the flappers, dappers, bright young things and delightful old fogeys who supported my Kickstarter.
Stay brilliant.

CONTENTS

1
LIVILLA

BEFORE SATURNALIS

NOX

I am angry.

I know what they think of me. Livilla Lord Wolf, Bitch of Aufleur.

They think I am hard and sharp and cruel.

They think I am frivolous and wasteful, that I haven't a thought in my head beyond what to wear and who to frig.

Even my lover: Garnet, the Power and Majesty. He does not see all of me. He sees the woman, and the wolves. He sees the frocks and painted mouth. He sees me bite, and watches me sleep.

He thinks I am his weapon to wield.

~

I LEAVE Garnet sleeping in our bed and walk out of the room naked, because I plan to shift my skin as soon as possible.

How to be human: you wear clothes and say witty things.

You go where you are told and fight the sky until it bleeds and the next day you get up and do it all over again.

How to be a wolf: the sky still needs fighting, but you don't worry about why. You simply are. (Being a wolf is the best thing that ever happened to me.)

I change into my favourite shape and I'm off, running the length of the underground ruin of a city where we make our home.

Here's one of my secrets: I can choose to be one wolf, or two. When we change our shape, we keep the same mass. In front of others, I choose to be two wolves because one can watch, and one can leap.

In our world, we pretend to be stronger than we are so that the others do not bite out our throats. As the only female Lord of the Creature Court, it's in my interest to be underestimated. If they truly knew the scope of my ambition, they would put me down without hesitation.

Garnet most of all.

When I am two wolves, I am sleek and delicate of feature. Sometimes one larger and one smaller; sometimes two medium-sized, clearly female wolves.

When I am alone, I walk on four paws. I let myself be huge: the mass of a slender and long-limbed human makes for an enormous wolf. I let myself be Livilla, the Livilla that I always wanted to be. Fierce. Proud. Powerful.

AFTER MY RUN, I don't return to Garnet's bed but my own, in the apartment below his balcony.

Here, my courtesi are asleep together with those of Warlord: greymoon cats and brocks and wolf pups. Ravens cover every high ledge in the room. Bats hang from the ceiling.

There's Warlord himself: my sweet Mars. Sleeping bare, the dark of his skin glowing against lamp-lit sheets. I slide out of my wolf-skin and into human shape, my own dark hair tumbling down my bare back. 'Shh, I'm here.'

He smiles, still half asleep, and rolls over to welcome me into his bed. 'Come and get me, then.' I should sleep. It's daylight and we need strength to fight the sky every nox. But Mars pulls me in, soft and hungry, and takes hold of my thigh with his broad hand. 'Livilla.'

This is my pack now; his and mine. I can never let go of Garnet (Garnet will never let go of me) but here with my Warlord and our courtesi, I am loved instead of owned. It's a strange sort of family.

Mars slides his mouth wetly over my breast, taking it into his mouth. Long, slow, luxurious licks. 'Livilla,' he says again.

'Yes,' I breathe back. Yes, to everything. Yes, I'm home.

NOX FALLS, and the sky falls with it.

I wake up with a shudder, half holding on to my bad dream. Then I realise that the bed is shuddering under me — the walls. The den.

Wolf pups leap at me, bouncing on the bed, forming themselves into the body of Seonard, fifteen years old and eager for battle. 'Is it time?'

I tie up my hair in a long loop with a favourite clasp. 'It's always time.'

No point in choosing clothes for the battle. I fashion myself into Lord form, stronger than any squishy human, all spiky power and muscles that could wrestle my wolf self to the ground. Beside me, Mars shapes himself into Warlord, his greater self, my equal. 'To me,' he growls and his courtesi gather to him still in their creature forms: cats and bats and brocks.

The ravens are mine. 'Janvier,' I call and he forms himself in a blur of black feathers into my rangy warrior.

'Can we go?' Seonard begs.

We leave in formation, swarming out of the den and down the tunnels towards the Lock that will release us into the city above and the sky, always the sky.

The sky is waiting to kill us.

ABOVE THE CITY, Garnet comes into his own as Power and Majesty. The Lords and Court flock to him, taking his orders, lending our power to his.

I can't fight the sky at his side without remembering what it was like a decade ago when we were as young as Janvier and Seonard are now.

Garnet and I had a different pack then. We served Tasha, our Lord of Lions, along with other courtesi: Ashiol, Lysandor (long gone, both of them) and the boy Poet. Tasha was glorious. She terrified me during daylight hours but when nox fell and the sky burned she was a saint and an angel; queen and princessa. I loved and hated her in equal measure.

I wonder if I'll ever be able to hold Garnet in my arms, and not think about the day that he killed her.

Up here at least I can think about our enemy. The sky does not have a voice, or a face. It sends crackling weapons of light and colour, brightness and texture. It would destroy our city if we were not here, biting and clawing, defending Aufleur.

Aufleur does not even know that we exist, that the war goes on, that they owe everything to us.

Finally the battle is over; hours before dawn. It was a good nox. No one is dead. My boys scamper away with Warlord and his courtesi. Garnet is nowhere to be seen but I know he's expecting me back at the Haymarket to pay court to him as Power and Majesty.

I fall out of wolf-shape and for one solitary moment I stand on the edge of the Cathedral roof, naked and shameless, watching the city we have saved. I let myself feel, instead of hiding beneath the layers of flirtation and threat.

I feel nothing.

Behind me, a roof tile scrapes and I feel the presence of a man I once thought of as a brother.

Poet is an enigma: barely into his twenties, he dresses as a fine seigneur and plays the showman, like he's a man twice his age. Even now, naked and exhausted from the battle, he builds his stage self with me as his audience. Chin up. Smile sweet. Eyes knowing.

'Hello, dearling,' he says.

'What do you want?' My voice is flat because I don't care, I don't want to put on a show. Let me be alone for a minute... for an hour. Can't I have a moment to myself?

'To save your life.'

I snap at him, impatient with his nonsense. 'Don't be so dramatic.'

'You're interested, though,' he murmurs. I've got your attention.'

'The battle's over, Poet. Go home to your lads.'

Poet has never been comfortable with the pecking order of the Creature Court: like me, he started off low as dirt. He never quite settled into being a Lord instead of a courteso. This year, he finally took on two courtesi of his own, the bear and the weasel. It's been good for him, I think. It keeps him tethered here, among us. I no longer watch him to see if this nox will be the one he chooses to run away from the city, or finally embrace a Death by Sky.

Only now does it occur to me that he has been watching me for those signs, too.

'You're in trouble,' he says in a low, urgent voice.

I brush him off. 'What are you talking about? I'm fine. I'm marvellous.'

'You're not happy, Liv. Do you think I can't tell the difference?'

'I have everything I ever wanted,' I hiss at him, and the lie is too big for either of us to swallow.

'There are three hours until dawn,' Poet says in the softest voice. 'Give them to me. I... need a favour.'

I raise my eyebrows, unimpressed. 'Which is it, doing you a favour or saving my life?'

He gives me his most angelic face. 'Can't it be both?'

2

NEPTUNALIA

THE KALENDS OF SATURNALIS

DAYLIGHT

S o this was Aufleur. Evanderline Inglirra stepped off
the train in her tweed coat and comfortable
culottes, gazing with an observant eye around the platform.
The newspapers she wrote for back home were always so
thirsty for snippets on Aufleur fashions and food and
"charming rituals." There was little evidence of the city's
infamous elegance here. Every traveller was wrapped up in
thick wool coats and their own affairs.

Barely a handful of women had their hair bobbed in the
new style; few hems inched anywhere near the knee-length
so popular in Laudinon this season.

If the city wasn't going to provide peacock demmes,
painted clowns with ornamental cigarette holders and
daringly trend-setting ankle-boots, what was the point of
Aufleur at all?

Evie moved briskly through the frosted streets, crossing
the river and leaving the dockland district in search of the

newspaper office. There was no snow, at least, which made this city preferable to hers. Laudinon would be a landscape of icy misery for some months to come.

The Forum was as grand and imposing as Evie had been led to believe, and here at least she saw some signs of the cutting-edge artisan fashion that so delighted the commentators across the Orcadian Strait. Looped brooches of pearl beading, pinning up sleeves and hair. Jewelled markings on wrists and throats, where a clever stole could quickly hide them from view. Highly impractical shoes.

Clearly this was where the mode gathered to admire each other's taste. The younger demoiselles flashed their feathers at each other. Some of the older cosmopolitan dames wore their hair pinned to give the illusion it was short, even if they dared not go the full "chop."

Corsetry was out for anyone under forty, so more than a quarter of the city's population could breathe easier than ever before.

Still, not one demme or dame in the entire city wore trousers as Evie did; she was beginning to suspect that this was a fashion faux pas.

~

THE AUFLEUR GAZETTE was about what Evie had expected; a seedy office of hacks and con-men rattling away at vintage typewriters. The air smelled of cigarette smoke, egotism and unwashed shirts. She planned to spend as little time here as possible, but it was important to keep them sweet.

Local credentials were effective when opening doors, and mouths. She needed everyone to remember her as the slightly scandalous, mostly respectable newspaper writer that she was, so that they didn't start suspecting any other reason for her visit to the city.

Jardin Falcone, the Gazette's editor, had some kind of long-standing friendship or rivalry with Evie's own editor back home, and had negotiated a tight syndication contract for the pieces she would write here. He was a stocky man in a suit too expensive for his own tastes: his jacket had already been tossed to the floor by the time Evie met with him, his sleeves rolled up and ink-stained.

This was a man who did not do his own laundry.

Evie knew how to deal with men like Jardin Falcone; she'd have the Aufleur Gazette eating out of her hand by the time she was done, from the ink boy to the printers.

For now, she smiled and nodded and kept aloof, knowing from the first meeting that Jardin Falcone was the kind of editor who felt it necessary to punctuate all business discussions with random touches to the shoulder, hip and hair.

ONCE EQUIPPED WITH A DESK, a promised tour of the printing factory she would never take them up on, and an official Aufleur Gazette bronzed badge, Evie swept out of the offices in search of that most essential element of a travelling writer: a reasonably-priced boarding house.

She had done her research. Aufleur was built around hills, and the rents grew higher along with the streets. The Lucian district, on the edge of the city with the busy River Verticordia wrapped around its backside, was where the bohemians of the demi-monde could afford to live: the bartenders, prostitutes, portrait-painters, drunken poets and, most relevant to Evie's own current interests, the theatricals.

If she wanted a respectable boarding house, Evie would have been better off looking in the Giacosa district, which was recommended by everyone she met. Half the population of Aufleur had an auntie in Giacosa with a room to let.

Evie wasn't looking for respectable. She needed a different kind of auntie altogether, to source a bed within comfortable walking distance of a high-end musette known as the Vittorina Royale.

Dame Gretchau (rooms for rent by written request) was a retired columbine dancer who had once performed at the Palazzo in front of the old Duc and Duchessa d'Aufleur, to great acclaim. She now owned several houses in the theatre district, one for each of her late husbands.

The street didn't have a name, four turns off Via Cinqueline, and it was so narrow that the lodgers of the building opposite could lean out their windows and pass a pot of tea across the alley. They collaborated with each other on laundry lines strung between the windows above Evie's head: bedclothes and tunics flapped in the air, along with the occasional bright flash of more intimate apparel.

She knocked several times, finally nudging impatiently at the bright blue-painted door that had not been latched properly. 'Hello? Is anyone home?'

The door opened into a narrow hallway, with rickety stairs leading skywards, and a heavenly scent of fresh bread and butter. There was a blood-curdling scream from above, and a thumping sound.

'I'll kill him!' cried a female voice, a second later, as Evie hovered on the threshold. 'I'll kill him and then I'll kill her and then I'll SING ABOUT IT!'

A whirlwind in a Camoiserian silk dressing gown, cherry-red hair and a matching camisole, flew down the stairs and out the front door, barefoot and furious. She tumbled directly into Evie, apparently without noticing her existence or that of her valise, which fell to the floor in the commotion. 'I'll eat his guts!' shrieked the harridan in beautiful underwear, and stormed away into the street.

Evie took a deep breath and recovered her valise.

'Well, hello,' said an amused voice. 'You're new.'

Evie looked up to see a beautiful young man leaning over the stair railing, his hair falling in his eyes. He was in his shirtsleeves and little else. 'I'm supposed to meet Dame Gretchau here, to collect my key,' she said uncertainly.

'She'll be drunk off her arse at the Fallen Stem, it's past midday,' said the young man carelessly. 'The Old Duck usually rolls in before noxfall.' He indicated the latched door of the lower apartment, which must belong to their landlady. 'No point waiting down here. Keep me company while I put my face on.'

His name was Christophe, and Evie was correct when she guessed he was one of the Vittorina Royale's company. She had chosen the right boarding house.

'I'm a dancer and a songbird, not a mask,' he insisted, the distinction important to him. 'Worked my way up to first harlequinus this season. A prime role, so they say, but it's mostly throwing demmes in petticoats about the stage, which I happen to be smashing at. '

'There are worse ways to make a living,' Evie considered as they climbed the stairs.

'Tell me about it! I have a bunch of odd jobs in the off season, to keep the Old Duck from kicking me out. Pouring drinks in The Bell and Whip-hand. Stitching wounds for the local dottore when his real assistant forgets to come home from The Bell and Whip-hand. Pouring drinks AND stitching wounds at The Tender Cove, where the tips are better but the bar fights are worse. Aufleur rents are getting steeper every season.'

'How long have you lived here?' Evie asked Christophe, who led her past the first landing ('Seigneur Marco has that room, don't bother him, he's deaf and handsy... that one was Lilibet's but she ran off to marry a sailor so I suppose it will be yours,') and the second landing ('that's me, I share a twin with Himself but you won't see him around much, he sleeps standing up in the theatre if he's not off with one of his fancy men') to an open sitting room with a tiny kitchen ('don't try to cook anything for saints' sake, we'll all go up in flames, but there's a dear little oil stove in the corner where you can boil water for tea or ciocolata, and the Old Duck lets us make toast downstairs when she's in a good mood').

'Do you have a show this nox?' Evie asked, placing her valise in the corner and accepting a lukewarm cup of ciocolata. Christophe then settled himself before an enormous mirror and a range of lip-paint, rouge and other types of cosmetick she'd never even heard of.

'Worse,' said Christophe with a groan. 'It's a party for benefactors. Himself likes to parade us around before a new season begins, lure in all the fancy sponsors to gawk at us like elephants in a parade. The food's not bad,' he added grudgingly. 'And the theatre's doing better since Himself took over, our last stagemaster almost ran it into the ground. But if you put that many actors in a room with toffs looking for an easy lay, there's always going to be wall to wall melodrama.'

Evie curled up on the faded couch. 'Himself is the stagemaster? The young one, taking the city by storm? They call him the Orphan Princel, don't they?'

Christophe gave her a narrow look, as if it only now occurred to him now to be wary. 'And what do you do, dearling? Dame Gretchau attracts all sorts around here, but we don't get a lot of Inglirrans in the theatre district.'

Evie had already made up her mind to be as truthful as possible. It was the best way to hide the important lies. It helped that her cover was based on a truth she had been establishing for years. 'I write for newspapers. Profile pieces and the like, though my specialty is serial stories.'

'The scandal dramas?' Christophe attacked his eyelids

with a heavy pencil. 'Highwaymen falling in love with pirates and what was that last one? Elegant vampires who pine after quivering maidens. Lovelorn glances and heavy petting, marvellous stuff.'

'That one was mine, actually.' Evie was rather proud of her vampire melodrama, not least because it featured lesbians that stayed alive all the way to the end of the story. Her vampire lesbians not only provided her with a legitimate stream of income to justify a trip like this, they gave her the perfect veneer of trashy artistic credentials.

'Get the frig out,' Christophe gasped. 'You wrote The Blood of Lady Wister? I loved that one. Ruby-red read portions of it out at parties. She wanted to be Ludmilla.'

'We all want to be Ludmilla,' Evie said dryly.

'I could have sworn it was written by a man. You're Evander X?'

'Evanderline Inglirra,' she said, using her travelling name, the one that marked out her country of origin. 'The readers will take any amount of bosom-ripping, but they draw the line at a demme earning coin for words.'

Christophe ran an eye over her with a smirk. 'Imagine if they knew you wore trousers.'

'Culottes are not even daring in some parts of Laudinon,' Evie protested, which was mostly true.

'What are you here to write about now? Us, I hope?'

Evie smiled to herself. 'Only if you think you can provide enough scandal.'

RUBY-RED, the shrieking maelstrom in silk sleepwear so expensive that she saw no issue in walking the streets of the city in it, returned to the boarding house an hour or so later, armed with a bottle of gin and the latest gossip.

She was accompanied by Sunshine, another of Dame Gretchau's tenants, who was introduced to Evie with they/them pronouns, a wicked smile and a bag of fresh limes.

'It's true,' said Ruby-red, pouring gin with a steady hand in frighteningly accurate measurements. 'He's brought in a new stellar for the Saturnalia season. Why are we only hearing about this now?'

'You're just cranky that it's not you,' said Sunshine, slicing and distributing limes as fast as Ruby-red could pour the gin.

'You'll never guess who it is,' said Ruby-red, looking as grim as if she was reporting on a daily list of executions. 'Talk about a blast from the past.' She moaned and shook her head. 'Why did Adriane have to run off with that dreadful moustache-salesman *now*, I swear I'd have taken her place if she'd waited another three months for me to perfect my original devil ballet.'

'He didn't sell moustaches,' said Christophe patiently. 'He sold health tonics and moustache *combs*. While sporting, it has to be said, the world's most extraordinary moustache. You could hang ribbons off that monster. Don't be bitchy. You'd run away from the theatre too if you fished up a seigneur with more money than sense. Some demmes will do a lot for three meals a day.'

'Hogwash,' said Ruby-red. 'Who eats three meals a day? See me giving up the stage for a gent!'

Evie, understanding that her role here was to be their audience, sipped her gin instead of swallowing it in gulps.

Sunshine noticed, and passed her extra limes to make it go further. At least no one was going to get scurvy in this city.

'You'll never guess who it is,' repeated Ruby-red, her outrage diluted by moustache talk and gin.

Christophe and Sunshine exchanged an uneasy look, the

kind that made it clear they had been friends a long time. They knew when a storm was brewing.

'You already know!' Ruby-red hollered in fury, slamming down her glass.

'Tell us anyway, pet,' urged Christophe.

'How do you know?' Ruby-red practically swooned with the betrayal.

'He trotted her around the theatre this morning to measure her for costumes, when you and Christophe were at breakfast with those mandolin players,' admitted Sunshine, muddling their gin back and forth in the glass. 'Nose in the air like she thinks she's the duck's quack. I'm not sure she's even agreed to it yet.'

'Oh, she'll be on that stage,' said Ruby-red in a hard voice. 'He has her name painted on the frigging dressing room door.'

'I thought Himself would take that dressing room,' said Christophe, knocking back his gin without disturbing his violet lip-paint. 'It's the best one, and it's not like he doesn't perform above the rest of us. He should be the fucking stellar, everyone knows it.'

'She's not anyone,' Ruby-red pouted. 'How can she come back after all this time and be head and shoulders above the rest of us? My voice was better than hers and I'm a columbine. I'm not going this nox. Not if she's going to be there, prancing around like a meringue. Himself can swing for it.'

'He ordered the good pastries from that place in the Lucretine,' said Sunshine thoughtfully. 'The ones with the figs and cherries.'

There was a pause, as they all considered the benefit of good pastries versus the torment of making nice to an old foe, or friend.

'I'll go for a bit,' conceded Ruby-red. 'Half an hour, tops.'

Christophe leaned into Evie. 'Enough melodrama for your story yet, Inglirra?'

'I'll admit I'm curious to see your theatre,' said Evie. 'And to meet Himself.'

'Careful he doesn't rope you into a job,' laughed Christophe. 'None of us planned to be still at the Vittorina Royale this season, but he talked us all into new contracts. I had offers from as far away as Orcadia,' he added, and his friends groaned as if they had heard this boast many times already

'Himself's still agonising over the saints-and-angel play,' said Sunshine. They gave Evie a considering look. 'Say the word 'writer' and he'll throw himself at your feet. Have you ever scribbled for the stage?'

'I'm not looking for another job,' Evie said quickly.

'It's a lot like the newspaper stories,' Christophe said helpfully. 'But more talking and fewer cliffhangers. Mind, I'd love to see you tie a lady to the train tracks before the intervale... do we have a painted dropcloth for a train station set, Sunshine?'

Ruby-red drew a breath.

Evie waited. If Ruby-red took against her, it would be harder for Evie to unroll a low-key entrance in to the world of Aufleur's theatrical crowd.

'I hope you have a pair of formal trousers in that little satchel of yours,' said Ruby-red.

Evie was going to take that as acceptance. 'I think I can pull something together.'

'Well, then,' said Ruby-red with an air of benevolence. 'You can come along, if you don't embarrass us.'

'That's hardly fair,' said Sunshine, their deep green eyes firmly fixed on Evie. 'Embarrassing ourselves is how you know we've arrived at a party.'

3

NEPTUNALIA

THE KALENDS OF SATURNALIS

NOX

*E*vie was invisible in this crowd of peacocks. By the time they reached the Vittorina Royale — of course the party was thrown in the theatre, where else would it be? — the small gang of performers from the house with the blue door had turned into a colossal troupe of painted faces, shimmering costumes, and daringly bare arms.

Evie's smartest velvet trousers and softly tied cravat were barely worth a gasp with Ruby-red wearing a gown slashed above the knee, and Christophe sporting more cosmetick than any demme in the room. They entered the theatre in a rumpus of laughter which drew attention away from the less experienced columbines and masks who had arrived at the party on time, instead of two hours late.

There was music from a live band, and green cocktail glasses that looked like they had been stolen from some Great Families house party.

Evie kept to the edges, observing the thrum. You could

see from the ebb and flow of people which attendees at the party considered themselves important: the patrons and sponsors in their stuffed shirts and matronly gowns, who considered themselves free to grope any member of the company who got close enough to be touched.

She knew this kind of people: the swells and toffs. She made most of her money from them in her other career, the one that lay hidden beneath the strategically layered identities of Evander X and Evanderline Inglirra.

Christophe and Ruby-red were the life of the party, darting this way and that, snatching and eating up food from the trays without appearing to partake.

The moon and stars around which they all spun was the man called the Orphan Princel, youngest stagemaster in a century. He was an elegant fellow in a gaudy bespoke suit that fit his slender figure devastatingly well. Evie already wanted the name of his tailor.

He arrived in a top hat and spectacles, with only a hint of lip-paint to help his smile carry to all corners of the room.

Once the soirée was warmed up with wine, grilled oysters and the pastries which were in fact the best thing Evie had ever put into her mouth, the music stilled and the stage-master leapt up to the stage to make a speech.

'Dearlings all,' he said with a grandiose bow. 'Happy Neptunalia! If you are here as our guest, you are part of the Vittorina Royale family. You are a Mermaid, and a Pearl Beyond Price. You will always be welcome within our walls… as long as you buy a ticket!'

The crowd laughed dutifully.

'The winter is frosting the tips of this city, and Saturnalia is just around the corner.' The stagemaster's tone was serious for a moment. 'A dark time. A month of chilled air, and sad thoughts of those we have lost. But…' And here he teased again, smirking at them all. 'Here at the theatre, we will always keep you warm, and bring you joy. Our new season will begin on the Ides of Saturnalis as is traditional for the Mermaid Revue, since before we found our home here, at the Vittorina Royale. I have the very greatest pleasure to announce that this year, for our Saturnalia season, the last and most important theatrical season of the calendar, we have a new stellar.'

Everyone buzzed wildly at the announcement. The stage-master stilled their speculations with one calculated hand. 'This lovely demoiselle has performed in every city of Ammoria, Orcadia and Atulia. She taught the savages of Nova Stella to dance, and made the Princessa of Isharo cry for unrequited love of her. Here, for one season only, on the finest stage of the finest theatre in the finest city of the world, the Vittorina Royale proudly hosts: Lady Livilla.'

The lights guttered, and lanterns flickered aflame only on the stage, framing the shape of the Orphan Princel and, in silhouette behind him, the band. A woman stepped out from behind the curtain, and stood at the stagemaster's side.

She was taller than him, graceful and every inch the fashionable beauty, with pale skin and black hair cut into a sharp, daring bob. Her mouth was a slash of scarlet, her eyes outlined with as much cosmetick as Christophe. She wore white: a modest fall of a gown sewn with seed pearls and satin fringe, to symbolise the angel of the saints-and-angel play, a cornerstone of Saturnalia entertainments. Her arms were adorned with far more bracelets than any respectable demme would wear in Laudinon, even in the theatre district where 'respectable' was a fantasy few cared about. Around her neck hung a single, perfect strand of pearls, six inches longer than any current fashion.

Lady Livilla did not sing, or dance, but gazed out at the crowd as if she wanted to bite all of their faces off.

'Oh,' breathed Christophe into Evie's ear, his breath heavy

with the ansouisettes he had been drinking. 'This is going to be magnificent.'

The music began again. The stagemaster led Lady Livilla around the gathering in a calculated parade, introducing her to the fanciest and richest of the theatre patrons.

When they swung past Christophe's crew, Evie saw the Lady's sharp face melt for the first time, as if she was a real person.

'Kip,' the stellar breathed.

Christophe smiled warmly and kissed her hand. 'Hello, Liv,' he said in a quiet voice.

Ruby-red barrelled out of the corner and threw herself at Lady Livilla, arms wrapping tightly around her neck in an embrace that startled everyone. 'I missed you, bitch,' she said in a muffled voice. 'Where the hells have you been?'

Lady Livilla's painted face softened further, into something quietly tragic. 'You wouldn't believe me if I told you, Rubes,' she said, hugging back until Christophe and Sunshine came forward to discreetly prise Ruby-red off her old friend.

The stagemaster's sharp bespectacled gaze fell on Evie. 'You're new,' he observed.

'This is Evander X,' said Christophe, slinging a casual arm around Evie's shoulders. 'She writes newspaper melodramas, but is looking for some local work. Plays, perhaps?'

Evie opened her mouth to protest because she was not even slightly looking for work let alone stagewriting, but the Orphan Princel was already weighing up her worth.

'Bring her to breakfast at Yvette's,' he commanded, and swept onwards with Livilla on his arm. 'Stay brilliant, my loves!'

4
ONE DAY AFTER THE
KALENDS OF SATURNALIS

DAYLIGHT

Breakfast for the theatrical demi-monde of Aufleur happened an hour before noon at the absolute earliest. Evie woke too soon, the winter sun blazing through the tiny window of her digs. She was going to have to train herself to be nocturnal, at this rate; she felt still half-drunk from cocktails the nox before.

According to local legend, which was to say, Christophe's love of gossip, Yvette Lebeau was a former courtesan of the late Duc d'Aufleur. She owned a sprawling house on the corner of the Marius Bridge over the River Verticordia.

'She never comes to our parties,' explained Christophe that morning, as they strolled alongside the river with Ruby-red, Sunshine and a handsome tumbler called Zephyr who had clearly spent the nox in Christophe's bed. 'But she throws more money at the Vittorina Royale than half our sponsors combined, and she always buys a box when a new season opens — it's about the only time she leaves the house.'

'She likes to have us visit to share our most scandalous stories,' said Ruby-red. 'I hope you have at least one spurned lover up your sleeve, Inglirra. Everyone is expected to sing for their supper.'

'Her cook is the best in the city,' said Sunshine gleefully. They wore a straw hat over their short curly hair, avoiding sunlight. This was their hangover cure of choice, and it looked far more appealing than Ruby-red's patented egg-and-vinegar concoction.

Evie wished she had known an hour ago she was allowed to beg a straw hat and reject the vile egg drink. Slowly, she was getting the measure of these people.

'I hope he's bringing Liv,' said Ruby-red with a skip in her step. 'Yvette will ferret out all her secrets.'

'Of course you know her from the olden days,' said Sunshine.

'Sunny likes to remind us they are younger and more innocent than us raddled old veterans,' said Christophe in a loud whisper. 'But they were dancing on street corners here in the city when we were learning our trade in a tiny seaside town... so really, how innocent could they possibly be?'

'Not that innocent,' Sunshine admitted with a smirk.

'She's glamorous as frig,' said Zephyr, trying to hold Christophe's hand, only to be shaken off like he was a puppy. 'What was she like back then, the Lady Livilla?'

'She's no lady,' Ruby-red sniffed. 'Ever seen a cabaret of monsters? We haven't had one of those for a few years around here, though Himself keeps promising to round up a new crop of lambs we can train into it. Liv was one of us, back then. Nothing special.'

Evie thought of what she had read up on about Ammo-rian theatre traditions. 'The cabaret of monsters, that's the one with children dancing in animal masks, isn't it?'

'I was a cat,' said Ruby-red with a toss of her pretty head. 'Of course, I'm a real performer now. Second columbine.'

'And that's good?' Evie guessed.

Ruby-red gave her a deathly expression. 'Yes, that's good.'

'It means she plays all the evil fairies and wicked sisters,' put in Christophe. 'Much better costumes than the prima columbine. Sometimes I even get to throw her around the stage.' He hooked his arm in Ruby-red's. 'Come on, minx. Stop picking fights. I'm starving.'

YVETTE LEBEAU WAS A CURVACEOUS, well-preserved middle-aged dame who wore head-to-toe satin, and a jewelled hair band that was entirely the mode. She welcomed in the bright young things and rapped out commands to her overworked maid from the position of a low, draped couch.

Her river house was a thing of faded beauty, all soft green frescos and mosaic floors, but freezing cold. Coming in from the morning sunshine, Christophe and his crew seized coats and blankets from a heap near the doorway, bundling themselves with warm layers in a practiced routine.

Yvette served a splendid breakfast of sardines, fried mushrooms and coronets. Evie had heard of these buttery lemon-glazed pastries before, but the lopsided crescents served in Laudinon teashops lacked the crisp saltiness of the authentic Aufleur version, shaped like crowns.

The theatricals fell on them like wolves, stuffing the pastry crowns with sardines, white slabs of cheese, or a sweet paste made of hazelnuts and almonds.

Yvette served leaf tea, a smoky variant that Evie had never tasted before.

Christophe and the others sang for their supper by

reporting scandals that surely must be embellished if not entirely false. Evie let the tales wash over her, waiting to hear about the main event — the latest melodrama surrounding the Vittorina Royale. To her surprise, though, no one said a word about the mysterious Livilla.

The young stagemaster himself arrived, an hour later than everyone else. He kissed Yvette on both cheeks before helping himself to a plate of coronets. The maid brought him a cup of tea, and blushed when he was charming to her.

'Well?' Yvette sighed happily. 'Haven't you put the cat amongst the pigeons, my sweet.'

The stagemaster choked on a crumb. 'That's … hardly accurate,' he managed, and swallowed a hard mouthful of tea to clear his throat. 'What have you heard?'

'She taught the savages of Nova Stella to dance,' said Yvette, her painted eyebrows raised to the ceiling.

'We haven't said a word!' protested Christophe, eyes wide.

'Pshaw, you think you are my only visitors? I hear things.' She gave the stagemaster a narrow look. 'Dangerous people you run with these days, my boy.'

'That's old news,' he scoffed. 'What do you want to know, you delightful nag?'

'Where did you find this new stellar of yours?' She tapped a porcelain saucer with her fingernail, clearly knowing the answer.

'She's an old friend. I needed to spice up the Saturnalia revue this year,' said Himself, ignoring the dirty look Ruby-red shot in his direction.

'And is she beautiful?' Yvette pressed.

'Not as beautiful as you,' he replied gallantly. 'Livilla has… pizzazz.'

'Oh yes, she's full of that,' Ruby-red muttered.

'I don't know why you won't admit it,' said Christophe, his own arch mockery fading for once. 'You're our stellar. We don't need another. The Orphan Princel numbers have been our biggest draw for years. We're waiting for you to take your rightful place.'

The stagemaster blinked, his eyes holding Christophe's for a moment. Then he shrugged it off with a laugh. 'Who has time for that kind of responsibility? Yvette dearling, what gossip do you have to share?'

They laughed and flirted together for the rest of the breakfast. The stagemaster spent half his time with his head in the dame's lap, chatting about past love affairs, shocking costume choices, and other flimsy matters.

Evie watched them all, these theatricals that thrived on artifice and melodrama. There was a closeness to them all, and a distance. She didn't quite have a grasp on it yet, how they all fit together.

Just as she thought she had escaped the stagemaster's notice altogether, he tilted his head and looked at her like he could see everything inside her skull. 'And you, Evander X. What are you doing here, in our fair Aufleur?'

'I'm following a story,' she said truthfully, holding his gaze steady with her own. This odd little man with his spectacles and pretty friends wasn't going to intimidate her.

'Plenty of stories around here to go round,' huffed Yvette with a laugh.

'But you're digging for something in particular,' the Orphan Princel pressed. 'Aren't you?'

Evie relaxed her gaze. She could not afford to have him see her as a threat, not yet.

'I'll know it when I find it,' she said.

He nodded as if this answer was satisfactory, and went back to chatting about the lusty antics of songbirds and tumblers.

Evie ran her gaze over Himself once he was no longer paying attention to her. His suit was of fine brocade. His hair

was immaculately styled, and even his hands were mani-
cured. This was a man who knew how to take care of
himself, and had the money to afford it.

What was he, under that suit of clothes? A tigris? A hawk?
If she had to guess she would say: a wolf.

5

SEPTIMONTIA (SACRIFICE OF THE SEVEN HILLS)

THREE DAYS BEFORE THE IDES OF SATURNALIS.

A market-nine passed. Rehearsals were held every nox, as the company polished and prepared their Saturnalia revue for the new season, working their established material around a new stellar, and other innovations.

Evie had a standing invitation to observe rehearsals. She went along quite often as it was a great source of entertainment. Her notebook was filled with more questions than answers about the young stagemaster and all the backstage angst from the Vittorina Royale. It would either make a steamy series of articles, or a highly unbelievable fiction serial; Evie had not yet decided.

Christophe continued to insist Evie would work wonders on the tired saints-and-angel script, which was a constant source of gripes among the company.

The stagemaster did not trust Evie enough to rewrite his script, which was of little account to her, as she wasn't the one invested in the idea. It would be useful, though, to have his trust. She had to find her way into his other life somehow, and befriending his housemates only got her so far.

Himself was never home, so Evie's immersion in his

group of friends felt like a waste… or it would if she wasn't having such a wonderful time. She was in too deep, but that was nothing new. Sometimes, to follow a big story, you had to climb inside and bare your throat.

The story she was after was huge, with extremely sharp teeth. A little caution was not unwarranted. She could bide her time.

She had attended many rehearsals this week, but Evie sent her apologies on the nox of the Septimontia and headed to her desk at the Aufleur Gazette instead. Time to burn a typewriter at both ends. She had deadlines looming, and even the clueless Jardin Falcone would get suspicious if she didn't submit something tasty.

Working this late at least meant she could avoid having to do anything about Falcone's wandering hands. Punching out her boss wasn't going to help her remain the right side of barely-memorable around here. Evie churned out three chapters of a new newspaper serial about highwaymen, and walked home by the light of sacrificial fires, burning atop every hill in Aufleur.

The boarding house was quiet when she finally made it home in the early hours, well past any respectable hour. She fell asleep on top of the bedclothes on her narrow cot with its bleached pale sheets, her mind still writing one last scene, and another, her fingers twitching at the memory of type-writer keys.

SHE AWOKE in the early hours to the sound of wolves howling in the street outside. There was no sleeping after that.

Evie staggered out of her tiny room and up the narrow staircase two floors to the parlour, in search of tea or gin or something to chase the shadowy thoughts out of her head.

She found Sunshine, awake by lantern light, leafing through a paper-thin magazine of watercolour illustrations. Christophe snored on the opposite couch, his lip-paint smeared, a half bottle of gin cradled in his arms like he was never going to let go.

'Rough nox?' Evie asked.

'Ugh,' said Sunshine, turning a page. 'Livilla ditched rehearsals yet again, and Christophe got into a screaming row with Himself about it.'

'Christophe,' said Evie, who couldn't imagine him getting into a flap about anything. 'Really, not Ruby-red?'

Sunshine snorted. 'Rubes said her piece, got drunk and fucked Christophe's boyfriend in the props cupboard. So an ordinary nox around here, really.'

'Scandalous.'

'Scandalous is ordinary.'

Evie liked Sunshine. They were a calm presence, compared to the histrionics that Christophe, Ruby-red and the stagemaster dragged with them into every room. 'What do you do in the show?' Evie asked now. She couldn't quite believe she hadn't asked before.

Sunshine gave her a quizzical look. 'I'm a mask.'

'So you act.'

'I speak the lines, it's not exactly acting. Pretty masks, voice-work and dramatic poses. I used to be a tumbler. I'm still bendy, but I got too old for all those rolls and flips.'

Evie scoffed. 'You're not old.' Mid twenties, she thought; not much younger than her.

'We're all old in *The Theatre*,' said Sunshine with a dramatic flap of their hands, and heavy emphasis on the words. 'We come into the life as lambs and burn out long before we're even old enough to drink and smoke and frig around.' Another pose: this one swooning back on the couch with a melodramatically frozen face. 'We stick with *The*

29

Theatre through bruises and muscle strain and broken hearts because it's our life. We can't imagine anything else. Well,' they added, with a more natural frown. 'Most of us can't.'

'Is that why everyone's furious about Livilla?' Evie couldn't help digging into the mystery. 'Because she left?'

'She gave up the life,' Sunshine corrected. 'For true theatricals that's… death.'

'Wasn't she swanning around all the theatres in Ammoria all this time? From what the stagemaster said…'

Sunshine snorted. 'Yeah, no. That demme hasn't been on a stage in a decade or more. No one's heard a peep from her since she vanished. Not Christophe and Ruby-red, not anyone. Himself was lying his arse off about her, and fine, we lie to the public all the time. But he's lying to us. That's why we don't trust her. Trust is everything around here, and Himself broke ours to bring her in.'

It was more words than Evie had ever heard from Sunshine before. 'You really care about him, don't you?' she said softly now. 'All of you do. Considering he pays your wage.'

Sunshine gave a bittersweet smile. 'The last stagemaster was a waste of space. Only interested in who he could screw, and how much money he could squeeze out of the box office to spend on drink. Once he died and Himself came in, well. It was different. Himself's one of us. Not just because he's about twelve,' they added slyly. 'He's a real theatrical. One of the greats. If he'd actually accept stellar billing, we'd die of pride. He's what makes the Vittorina Royale great.'

It was a good story. It wasn't the whole story. Evie was a born muckraker; she knew where to dig for the good shit. 'But…' she encouraged.

Sunshine gave her a cynical look. 'What, you haven't got enough for your tell-all story yet?' They stood up and stretched, then prised the half bottle of gin from the snoring

Christophe and poured even measures into two tin mugs.
'He loves us but he's not always here,' they admitted, passing
one of the mugs to Evie. 'Especially after sundown. That's
why he won't let himself be our stellar. He draws crowds —
they buy tickets hand over fist to see him perform. But he
takes smaller parts and limits his solos because he can't
always guarantee to turn up. There have been shows, really
important shows, where Himself didn't turn up at all, or he
vanished before curtain call. He's never missed a daylight
matinee, but someone else has half his attention after dark.'

Evie considered the possibilities. 'A hidden family,
perhaps? A wife?'

Sunshine snorted. 'Three high maintenance boyfriends in
different districts, maybe. Not a wife. He's not that good an
actor. It doesn't matter why. The point is, he's not here. And
now he's landed us with a stellar who's equally unreliable.'
They shook their head impatiently. 'Don't mind me, I'm
bitching because I'm tired. Why are you awake this late?'

'Wolves,' said Evie, too tired to guard what she said. Gin
was lethal in the early hours. She wanted another. 'I heard
something like wolves outside.'

'Oh,' breathed Sunshine. 'I heard them too. I thought I
was dreaming. Some yahoo, I expect, messing around in the
street. Wolves in the city is not very likely, is it?'

'And yet,' said Evie in a low voice.

Sunshine met her gaze steadily. 'And yet.'

EVIE MADE her way to bed again, careful on the dark stairs,
promising herself she actually would sleep this time, and not
light the lantern to scribble thoughts about wolves.

She lit the lantern anyway, once the door was latched
behind her.

A shape loomed up out of the shadows by the window. Not human. Evie swallowed her own scream as she realised it was indeed a wolf.

A wolf in her bedroom. It was enormous, a husky creature with thick fur and deep, unblinking yellow eyes. It snarled, and blood dripped from its jaws on to the floorboards. Too much blood.

The wolf threw its head back with a yelp and then it wasn't a wolf any more. It had shaped itself into a demoiselle with bobbed hair. Her skin was milky white, almost too pale to be real. She was naked and bleeding from a wound punched through her entire chest.

'Livilla,' Evie breathed, recognising the demme.

This was it, the secret story of this city. The thread she had followed here, the one she had dug through the red velvet curtain of the Vittorina Royale to find. The whispered fairy tale was true.

In Aufleur, there were people who could transform into wolves.

Livilla coughed up fresh blood, wiping it from her mouth with an elegant hand. She shuddered, clutching her bleeding chest, and then fell apart into pieces.

She was two wolves now, both of them hurt, sprawled on Evie's floor.

Evie was long past screaming now. Instead, she began to laugh.

6
LIVILLA

※

BEFORE SATURNALIS

NOX

*F*or a long time now, I've known that the sky will kill me. This city will kill me. I will die at the hands of our nameless enemy or…

Or, let's be honest, I will die at the hands of a man. I share my bed with monsters. Sooner or later one of them will go too far and leave me in a crumpled heap on the floor.

On the whole, I would prefer it to be the sky. Why not die a hero, as one last cruel joke on a city that has never been kind to me?

I never expected it to be the theatre that killed me.

~

I DON'T RECALL a state of innocence. Growing up in a theatre, even a backwater hall like the Mermaid back home, innocence was a luxury no one could afford.

I spent my early years performing in the cabaret of

monsters, a chorus of masked children beloved in pantomimes and musettes. I wore many faces; it all depended which animal you snatched up on the day: I flitted between mouse, cat, gattopardo, rat, bird, ferax, wolf.

The wolf was my favourite, a moulded leather mask that smelled sometimes of peppermint, because it was also Rafaelo's favourite, and he was the biggest so got his pick more often than not. Later, when he went off to train as a tumbler, I secured the wolf mask as my own.

Being the wolf made me bigger, too. Made me strong. As the wolf, I could bite and dance and take as many helpings as I wanted for dinner.

As a child, that was all I wanted from life.

There were ten of us, lambs in the cabaret, and we knew how good we had it. Not everyone was lucky enough to be kept on with the company once they were too old to wear the animal masks. So we learned to tumble and dance and sing in our spare time. We made friends with the grown ups, treading that careful line between 'useful' and 'ambitious.'

For the demmes, there was another risk hanging over our heads as we grew older. No one wanted to capture the eye of the stagemaster.

NOW I'M on the roof with Poet, and he says those chilling words to me, 'You're not happy, Liv,' and what am I supposed to make of that?

Happy isn't a state I have thought much about, in recent years. I've been fighting to survive. I'm part of another cabaret of monsters now, a real one. In the Creature Court, we shape ourselves into wild beasts, and fight the sky to save the city.

I have never been stronger than I am now. Lord of

Wolves. I have my courtesi to adore and serve me. I share Garnet's bed when he summons me; I crawl in with Mars (Warlord, we call him Warlord now) and our pack (his courtesi and mine, together in a pile) when I want to feel safe.

I am beautiful, I have all the dresses I could ever need to wear, and my belly is always full of meat.

'What does happy even mean?' I ask Poet. I'm swaying now, on the very edge of the Cathedral. If I fell from this height, I would not die. I would burst apart into wolf shape, and run to safety.

I will not fall.

Poet and I haven't been friends for years. Our Lord of Rats has been too busy growing up into an elegant, dangerous stagemaster, perfecting his showman's face for a crowd of strangers.

I have been keeping on Garnet's good side, so he never does to me what he did to others we loved: so I don't end up exiled or broken or bleeding out on the floor of the Haymarket.

'Livilla,' says Poet now, and his hands are cool on my waist as he draws me back from the edge. 'You can't go on like this. Your courtesi are fretting over you. Warlord is fretting. Even I'm fretting, and I don't give a damn whether you live or die.'

I laugh at that. Foolish child. 'Back at you,' I whisper.

Poet turns his face into my neck like he used to when he was little, and I was big enough to shield him from the cruelty of Tasha, Lord of Lions, who made us what we are. 'Garnet will notice eventually. You can't let him see any weakness.'

'I'm not unhappy,' I protest. 'I'm not...' I don't feel anything. That's normal, isn't it?

'Please. For my sake. Find something for yourself. For one market-nine. One festival. Let yourself be Liv again.'

That's a startling thought. It tastes like daylight. 'What do you have in mind?'

Poet smiles at that. He's not handsome, not really. A funny looking boy, he grew up into a skinny young man with an odd face. He is beautiful in stage makeup and fine clothing; he uses his body as an instrument and if he wants you to love him, you will. You can't help yourself.

The theatre has eaten him alive, in recent years, but he wears it well.

'It's Saturnalia, dearling,' Poet croons. 'Everything is upside down and back to front. I want to take you off the street and put you back on the stage.'

'What,' I say lightly, turning it into a joke. 'Are you going to make me a stellar, Boy?'

'You're already a stellar, Livilla,' Poet says to me, deadly serious. 'I won't make you anything. But first things first.'

I frown. 'What do you have in mind?'

He tugs on the long tail of my dark hair, forcing it out of its pearl clasp, a pretty trinket my Janvier gave me last Floralia. 'A new look for a new year, dearling. Haven't you heard? Long hair is for Duchessas and old fogeys. If you're going to stand on my stage, I need a good-time demme with stars in her eyes and a song in her feet.'

'I'm a wolf, not a flapper.'

Poet smirks at me. 'Can't you be both?'

I WORE my hair short at the Mermaid, in the old days. It made me look younger, even when my legs sprouted, and fellows started to look up my skirt.

Ruby-red, my best friend backstage, had her eye on the columbine line. She shared her rations with me so she'd stay thin as a swan, and practiced her arches and stretches wher-

ever the adults could see her. She grew her hair long so she
could wear it up in a crown of roses.

We were both eleven when the company moved from our
tiny fishing town to play a big city theatre in Aufleur: Ruby-
red bounced with glee, thinking this was her big chance. She
meant to be a stellar by the time she was sixteen; as for me, I
had nowhere else to be. My brothers and cousins had never
known what to do with me after Ma died, and the theatre
was the best home I'd ever known.

By the time it sank in that we weren't just visiting
Aufleur, we were to stay at the Vittorina Royale as long as
our shows sold tickets… well, by then, our stellar was dead,
and the stagemaster already fucking the next one. He groped
the columbines openly, and called any demme of the
company to his office for a 'private chat' any time he fancied.

Everyone was at it: the tumblers, the masks, the songbirds, the stagehands. They were all half in love (or lust) with
each other. The roles they played on stage fed into backstage
drama and cheating, frantic frigging and face-slapping and
impulsive falling in and out of beds like a game of musical
chairs.

In retrospect, this prepared me well for my life in the
Creature Court.

There was casual nudity, too: no one turned a hair about
where they got changed backstage, or any other kind of
privacy. If you lived and worked at the Vittorina Royale, you
knew all the gossip and you'd seen half of it happen right in
front of you.

They did their best, most of them, to protect the lambs
from the drama and the fucking; one time we had a stage-
hand who tried to touch up Kip behind the canvas store, and
three tumblers went after him with a length of wood. While
we were young enough to wear the animal masks, we were
supposed to be safe.

Once you graduated out of the cabaret of monsters, assuming you still had a job, you were fair game. I know for a fact that Ruby-red spent three hours alone with the stage-master before he promoted her to columbine, and she wasn't even thirteen yet.

'Make up your mind, Liv,' she said once, though she barely spoke to me at all any more, now she was a columbine and fancying herself something chronic. 'Find a place for yourself or one day you'll wake up and you won't belong here.'

I wasn't good enough to be songbird, or dedicated enough to be a dancer. I could wear a mask well enough, though the parts for demmes were boring if you didn't sing and dance as well. I started to worry I would lose my place to someone younger, thirstier, more willing to sacrifice everything to be in the show...

But I found a different thirst altogether. A whole new mask to wear. That was when everything changed.

～

MY HAIR FALLS to the ground in clumps. I haven't cried in years; this won't break me. Last nox I bled all over the grass of the Gardens of Trajus Alysaundre, before the Sentinels came to do their damned job and fix my wounds by offering their throats to my teeth.

It's a black waterfall, hair sliding over my shoulders and hitting the ground in a swish. Poet perches on a bench nearby, watching with that critical eye of his.

The barber — a seigneur's barbershop, what has my life become — whistles between his teeth as he clips me raw.

'What have you done?' I whisper.

Poet leans in, eyes gleaming like he wants to ravish me,

which is all kinds of disturbing. Possibly he just wants to ravish my new haircut.

'Look at you!' he crows. 'The audience will eat you up!'

It occurs to me, too late, that Garnet might hate it. He's been erratic lately, our Power and Majesty. He can't stand feeling out of control and here I am, turning myself into someone new. Someone bold. A demme who bobs her hair.

'No regrets!' Poet commands.

'You say that,' I snap back. 'When has following you ever been a good idea?'

He taps me on the nose. 'Don't bite.'

If I went wolf, right here in the barber's chair, I could eat his throat out. He would taste delicious.

BEFORE HE WAS POET, our Boy disappeared. He was still young enough to play the cabaret of monsters for a good few years, so it was odd, but we were living in a big city now. Perhaps he'd been murdered, or sold to chimney sweeps. All our shows had songs about orphan boys who fell on their feet. No one was especially worried about him, except Kip who cried for days.

One day, he came back, just when I needed him most, and led me a fine old dance, to the Creature Court and our brand new life.

Moon blood doesn't mean much, though many try to build it up as a milestone in a demme's life. The first few spots I found in my linens filled me with terror because that was it, the beginning of the end. The cabaret of monsters wouldn't have me any more, if I was turning into a dame.

Hiding away in shabby over-sized tunics didn't stop me being leered at or groped. It was time to accept a different sort of armour.

Ruby-red helped me find the dress, a pretty floor-length thing with rosebuds all over in cheap lace. (In my memory it was fringed at the knee but that can't be right, that fashion didn't come in until later)

'You'll have to grow this out,' she said, tugging on my dark curls. There was no time for that now, so she pinned a loose ribbon cap to my scalp, with false hair falling out the back.

The gown was a deep lavender, and Ruby-red painted my face like I was the stellar herself, not some scrap of a lamb hoping to make it as a songbird.

'He don't do much,' Ruby-red assured me, about the stagemaster. 'He's all fumble and jiggle that one, and he always finishes on the outside.'

Adriane, our stellar, was days away from giving birth, and so furious she had to be replaced for the Saturnalia pantomime this year that she was constantly screaming and hollering. It wasn't true about the stagemaster always finishing on the outside. A baby was always a possibility, when men fumbled at you.

'It'll be over before you know it, and you'll have your place,' Ruby-red said, giving me a sisterly hug. It was the nicest she had been to me all year.

You'll have your place.

My stomach had cramped up all day, I thought from the moon blood. But it tightened and twisted all down my thighs to my ankles, as I knocked on the door of the stagemaster's little office up above backstage.

As soon as I stepped inside, I felt stupid. Ugly. The cosmetick on my mouth tasted awful. The stagemaster looked at me like I was a child playing comedy dress ups.

'Hello, Liv,' he said with a smirk. 'I hear you want to be a songbird.' He leaned back from the desk with a sigh, patting his knee.

I saw how it was going to go in that instant, unwinding

before me like a ribbon. I'd been so busy *not* thinking about what it meant to let him paw at me, to let him own me.

He paid the coin, he provided the roof, and we followed his rules: filled his shows, entertained his audiences, made his theatre grand and fine and beautiful.

I lifted my chin, forgetting about the dress and the cosmetick and everything else. I'd been in the chorus long enough that I could play a role if I had to, and the role I chose today was Lady Muck. 'No,' I told him.

He humphed. 'What? Think you can make it as a mask, scrawny mutt like you? You haven't got the grunt to be for a columbine, that takes a special something. Don't see you as a songbird, either. No lung capacity.' He made a crude gesture with his hands about how much he thought I had up top, which had nothing to do with my lungs. 'So tell me, little Liv. How are you gong to make yourself useful around here? Why the hells should I keep feeding you?'

He eased a hand into his trousers, not taking his eyes off me.

'I want your job,' I told him. 'I want to be stagemaster.'

He laughed at me, a big wet smacking laugh, and in that moment I was so furious at him that I...

Growled.

It was a deep, vicious sound from low in my belly, and it widened his eyes. For one brief moment he looked scared of me. I liked that. But then he went red in the face and got to his feet.

'If you won't pay your way,' he snarled. 'What use are you?'

I didn't even see him pick up the chair, but I felt the pain as it crashed into me, knocking me to the floor.

'What the fuck are you *for*?' he thundered, and hit me again.

It hurt, but I liked it, because the pain fed my anger, and

for the first time in my short, frustrating life, it felt like my anger was allowed.

He hadn't bothered to button his trews up; he was spilling out of them, and it looked like hitting me did more for him than anything I might have done with my mouth. He cupped himself with a hand; made a few rough jerks like he was preparing for action.

I didn't just growl this time; I roared. I thought about that leather mask, the one that had always made me feel strong like a wolf. I got to my feet, body aching, and I howled at him.

The stagemaster stumbled back, confused and startled. His hard-on sagged, and his hand fell to his side.

'If you touch me, I will kill you,' I said very calmly, and left the room. On the stairs, my legs shuddered as if I was about to collapse, but I couldn't let myself.

Behind me, I heard something smash against the wall, like he was doing to the chair what he had wanted to do to me.

I ran, and kept running. Down the stairs, out and out. My arms and legs hurt like the blazes, though I could barely feel the bruises. This was something else. My belly ached with hunger. I was angry and exhilarated, burning up as I scampered out to the alley behind the theatre. My muscles were on fire. No one had ever told me moonblood pains could be this bad. I hung on to the wall, heaving like I was about to throw up my guts.

Something else happened instead.

I shuddered and screamed and fell apart into wolf pups.

'It's all right,' Boy told me when he found me later, before he took me to the Creature Court, to Tasha and Garnet and Ashiol. Before he changed my life forever. 'Everything's going to be all right now, Liv. You're one of us. That means you have a pack. A family. It's better even than the theatre.'

I scoffed at him, even as my blood thrilled with the

change, with the new power I had found inside myself. What could be better than the theatre?

'You'll never be lonely again,' he promised me, and it was true enough at the time.

I AM the Lord of Wolves, and I have a place in the Creature Court. I have my pack, my lovers, my courtesi. I fight a war against the sky every nox. I am powerful. I am beautiful. I am loved.

I have never felt so lonely in all my life.

7

TWO DAYS BEFORE THE
IDES OF SATURNALIS

THE EARLY HOURS

'Y ou know,' said Christophe fervently. 'This
explains so much.'

He was the only one in the boarding house
with wound-stitching skills, thanks to his odd jobs as
bartender and dottore's assistant both.

Christophe used bright peacock-coloured thread to close
Livilla's angry wound. Sunshine and Evie stood back near
the doorway of Evie's room, both of them trying not to peer
too closely at the visceral details.

Every so often Livilla gasped and flailed and turned into
either one large or two smaller wolves, also wounded.
Christophe insisted on sewing them up as well, though he
asked Evie and Sunshine to help with that part, bracing
themselves with towels and blankets to hold the wolves
down.

They used gin to clean the wounds, and made Livilla
drink some when she was in human shape, to numb the pain.

Ruby-red, climbing out of her bed long after the others had run to answer Evie's cries for help, took one look at the messy scene and stormed out of the house, claiming she was going to locate Himself if she had to scour every bar in the city.

'What I'm hearing is, she thinks we might run out of gin,' Sunshine said dryly.

'The fear is real,' Evie drawled back.

She wanted to scream, and laugh. She'd faced dangers before, all kind of strange sights, in the work she never discussed with anyone but paying clients. Still, she'd never seen this before. It was new and exhilarating and terrifying.

How many of them are there in this city?

Sunshine took her hand, and Evie let them. If ever there was time for a bit of comforting hand-holding, it was this.

FINALLY THERE WAS A MENDED, bloodstained demme lying asleep on Evie's bed. Christophe, Evie and Sunshine sat around with the last of the gin, trying to make sense of recent events.

'I thought it was crime,' Christophe admitted, his head lolling against Sunshine's shoulder. 'You know. He has to get his money from somewhere. He was a bag of rags with nothing when he ran away as a lamb, and he came back years later as Lord Muck in A Top Hat, ready to save our souls with his deep pockets. It had to be a rich lover, gambling, gangsters, or all three. And there were times…'

'He looks hollow some days,' Sunshine added. 'Scraped raw. Like he's seen devils and angels, looked them right in the eye. Half the padding in his suit is secrets.'

'Do you think,' said Evie, and took another drink. 'Do you think he turns into wolves?'

The others considered this question in silence. She couldn't let them know how important the answer was to her.

Someone at the Vittorina Royale — someone who had been there longer than Livilla, was a thread connecting to the fairy tale creatures of the city, the people who turned into wolves. It had to be Himself. Didn't it?

There was a flurry at the window, and a bang. All three of them jumped and yelped with a varying degree of shrillness.

'That took fucking years off my life,' said Christophe, with a hand to his chest.

'Don't open the window,' Sunshine said urgently.

Evie stood on shaky feet and stepped closer. Shadows fluttered at the glass, pitch black outside their circle of lantern light. 'I think it's a bird,' she said, and took another step nearer the glass.

SLAM!

Ravens threw themselves at the glass, three or four of them. More. Evie saw a whole crowd of them — a murder, that was the collective noun. A murder of ravens. They swirled and swooped outside her window, crashing into it head-first as if desperate to come inside.

'What the fuck was in that gin?' Christophe asked wildly.

Livilla gasped and sat up. The thin blanket fell aside, baring her blood-stained breasts to the room. Her cosmetick was smeared. Her hair was a mess. 'Let him in,' she said. 'Open the window.'

'Uh, no,' Evie snapped. 'I'm not doing that.'

Livilla's eyes blazed a piercing blue all of a sudden, then bright golden yellow. She curled her lip up into a snarl. 'Open the frigging window.'

'How about you explain —' Christophe started.

Livilla screamed. She threw back her head and screamed

in a sound so sharp and desperate that it made the house shake.

The door burst open and Himself stood there. The stage-master. A narrow, gangling young man with spectacles, messy hair and a suit far too tailored and expensive to make any sense.

He has to get his money from somewhere, Christophe said.

Half the padding in his suit is secrets, Sunshine said.

Evie was pretty sure she knew one of those secrets.

'Calm down, dearling,' said Himself, as if finding a screaming, blood-stained, naked Livilla in another demme's bed was an ordinary market-nine for him. 'I've got your boys.'

He opened the door wider, with an actor's flourish. A horde of slithering, furry creatures tumbled over his feet, across the floor and up into Livilla's lap.

Weasels. What was the collective noun for weasels? If ravens were a murder, then weasels were... a scamper? A trick? An infestation?

Evie didn't realise she had spoken those words out loud until Himself answered: 'A confusion of weasels. Or a good old-fashioned pack. But you're right about ravens. They're a murder.'

Before Evie — before anyone — could stop him, Himself marched across the room and threw open the window.

Ravens flocked into the small space, flapping and cawing. Christophe yelled and batted at them. Sunshine sat down on the floor in a hurry, eyes wide and startled.

The ravens were here for Livilla. They blanketed her and the confusion of weasels with black feathers and angry eyes.

'Nope, I'm out,' said Christophe, and staggered out the door on wobbly legs.

Sunshine made a small moaning sound.

'Give us the room,' said Himself, with an imperious gesture.

Evie narrowed her eyes. She wasn't one of his cabaret kickers, and it was past time he remembered that. 'I don't take orders from...'

'Nope,' said Sunshine, bolting to their feet and slinging an arm around Evie's waist. 'Come on. You can bunk in with me.'

Evie sputtered, but allowed Sunshine to drag her out of the room, slamming the door on the chaos of animals and blood and secrets.

'What the fuck are you doing?' Himself screamed, on the other side of the door.

'This is our life, Poet, what do you want from me?' Livilla screamed back at him.

'Basic survival instincts, at a bare minimum! You were sloppy in the sky and you know it. I haven't seen you fight that badly since you were fourteen. Are you trying to end up dead?'

Evie wanted to keep listening, to learn as much as she could about what was going on here (Poet, she knew that name, she had been listening out for that name since she first arrived in the city) but the screaming devolved into muffled talking, and what might have been sobbing.

She startled as she felt Sunshine's hand on her arm. 'That offer was genuine,' said the theatrical. 'Come to bed with me.'

Evie kept staring at the closed door. Sleep. She did need sleep. Also, she needed to wash spatters of Livilla's blood off her skin. 'I don't want to put you out,' she said absently. 'I can crash in the upstairs parlour.'

Sunshine sighed. 'Let's blame the gin for how slow you are,' they said. 'No worries if you're not interested, but are you absolutely sure that you heard the invitation?'

Oh. Not bed, but *bed*. Evie heard a muffled thump from

within her room. More talking, but no more screams. She was exhausted, and wrung-out from the adrenaline, the shocks and the gin. She had a story to dig for, but it didn't have to be right this second.

'That's tempting,' she said, turning to look directly at Sunshine, whose eyes were dark in the barely-lit hallway. They hadn't brought the lantern with them, though Evie was certain that whatever Himself and Livilla and their animal friends were, they could all see in the dark...

Sunshine pressed into her, soft lips brushing Evie's mouth like a promise. 'Be tempted. Untangle the nonsense in the daylight.'

'That's the most sensible thing I've heard all nox.' Evie kissed Sunshine more thoroughly, embracing this welcome distraction from whatever was going on in her room. 'Who says I care enough to untangle the nonsense in the daylight?' she added.

Sunshine rolled their eyes. 'Please. I've slept with writers before. I know your kind.'

~

HOURS LATER, Evie startled awake from a sleep deeper than she had expected. Sunshine was a warm shape of limbs and hair beside her.

Why had Evie woken up? What kind of creature was invading the boarding house now?

She peered across the attic. Daylight sparkled through cracks in the shutters that Sunshine and Ruby-red kept closed, because they slept until nearly noon. Ruby-red was asleep in the narrow bed on the far side of the attic, along with another shape buried under quilts. Evie could only hope that it was not Zephyr, as there was enough drama around here already.

A knocking from below resounded up through the thin walls. A visitor on the doorstep. That must be what woke her up.

Evie borrowed an oversized silk coat from a heap of garments that almost certainly belonged to Ruby-red and not Sunshine (who kept better care of their things), and made her way downstairs, tying the sash securely around her waist.

No one else stirred as she made her way down. Christophe's door and Evie's were securely latched shut. Must she break down her own door to reclaim residence from Livilla and Himself?

First things first. Evie opened the door to find herself faced with... well, he had to be what Christophe always referred to as A Theatrical. A beautiful man, all blazing red hair and pale skin. He had a swagger to him, and a coat that might have been fine and fashionable years ago, but was worn and ragged at the seams.

'Livilla,' the stranger said in a rough voice. 'Where is she?'

Evie stood her ground. She'd lived in enough boarding houses over the years to know when you didn't let a demme's fancy man through the door, not with a set to his shoulders that told you he knew how to throw a punch. 'Never heard of her.'

'Evanderline,' said a soft voice at the top of the stairs. Himself stood there in his shirt and braces, still blood-stained from the nox before. 'Let him in. He's one of us.'

'He's safe?' she asked without thinking.

The visitor raised his eyebrows at that. Himself gave a hollow laugh. 'Not especially,' he said. 'But Livilla will want him, all the same.'

The dangerous man slid up the stairs like he was the stagemaster, and Himself was the servant who polished his boots. They stood together for a moment, murmuring, and then Himself took the man's hand, and led him into the room with Livilla.

As the door closed, Evie breathed out all at once. She felt like she had been punched, like she had been trapped in a room with a wild animal and only just escaped by the skin of her teeth.

She would like to say she had no idea why her body was alert with fight or flight, but the truth was... she had a very good idea who it was she had let into this house.

Evie hurried up the stairs, quickening her step as she passed her own landing, and kept going all in a rush until she was back in Sunshine's bed, burrowing under the quilts.

'What's the bother?' Sunshine muttered sleepily.

'Nothing,' said Evie. 'Shut up and kiss me.'

Sunshine smiled in the shuttered light, and wound soft arms around Evie's neck. 'That, I can do.'

LATER THAT DAY, the Mermaid Revue of the Vittorina Royale presented its final dress rehearsal of their Saturnalia show. They went through the afternoon and into the evening, every act performed twice.

Evie took absent-minded notes for her newspaper story as Christophe and Ruby-red blazed up the stage in the harlequinade, bouncing off each other with superb comic timing in a sea of trilling dancers. Christophe was the sad clown who loved the first columbine, a princessa in sugar-pink layers of petticoat. Ruby-red played the wicked fairy who kept the lovers apart by repeatedly enchanting them to fall in love with all manner of strange creatures played by tumblers in garish masks.

The love-dance of Harlequino and the donkey was something to be seen. Evie had watched it before, but never with the comedy mask in place; it made her laugh out loud.

She couldn't quell the thought that she had done something wrong that morning. She should not have let that strange man into the house where Livilla was so vulnerable.

Would Livilla even make it to the rehearsal? Her performance was up next. Surely she wouldn't be up to climbing out of bed, with her belly so recently stitched.

'We're almost there,' said a low voice, at Evie's ear. She did not have to turn to know Himself sat behind her, observing the rehearsal with a very different eye to hers.

'It's brilliant,' she said honestly.

'Mmm.' He didn't sound impressed. 'Tell me what we're missing.'

Evie's fountain pen tapped against her notebook. 'Well. There's the rather obvious absence.' She did turn this time, giving him an arch look. 'You have friends who can turn into animals. Why isn't that in your show?'

Tumblers spun and rolled across the stage, wearing masks of cats and hounds, ferax and lions. Not a cabaret of monsters in the traditional sense, because they weren't played by children. But it made a spectacular segue to the saints-and-angels play.

'What makes you think it's not?' asked Himself.

The stage cleared, and Livilla stepped out in the gown of an angel, trailing white feathers and strands of star-beads across the stage.

Evie stared. How was she even upright?

It was a beautiful song; the angelic interlude was a classic piece of stagecraft. Behind her, the saints and other masks fell into place, tugging props and set pieces as they went, preparing for the final act.

Sunshine, who had already performed two solo skits with great humour and grace throughout the show, was on stage now in a silver mask. They played the wicked, charming saint to Livilla's exquisite angel… the two of them flirted archly from stage left to stage right and back again, making the play far more sensuously charged than an audience might expect.

In the traditional story, saints were tempted by the angel, who literally seduced them into treading the path of virtue, only to draw swords in the final scene and send them off to war in the name of goodness and sacred duty. Here, it seemed that the opposite was happening. Sunshine the saint, with their army of sidekicks and cat-faced tumblers, was always one line of song away from corrupting Livilla's angel quite completely… while Livilla, eyelashes fluttering, seemed utterly delighted to be corrupted.

'What would you change?' Himself pressed. 'About the saints-and-angel?'

'It's a little late for notes,' said Evie. 'The show opens to the public in two days.'

'It's never too late,' said the stagemaster.

'He must have been quite a dottore,' Evie said under her breath, as Livilla swept gracefully into stage left, her head held high. 'The cove you brought to her room this morning,' she added. 'You'd never know she was wounded at all.'

'Oh,' said Himself, mouth going thin. 'He wasn't a dottore. Rather the opposite.'

THE DRESS REHEARSAL was enough of a triumph that the cast and crew demanded a celebratory breakfast, despite it being well into the evening.

Livilla was invited along, and almost looked like she was going to join them, but the gentleman in the ragged coat and dangerous eyes turned up again, with a bouquet of flowers that Himself looked at furiously, as if he wanted to stomp them to the ground.

'Garnet,' laughed Livilla, clasping the flowers to her bosom. 'You shouldn't have.'

Garnet, of course. Evie watched him from where she stood, surrounded by theatricals. She had guessed it was him, but knowing it for certain... that was something else.

He didn't look much like a murderer, but Evie knew better than most that you could never tell *that* from a person's outside appearance. He was pissed off and demanding, all the same. 'Poet, are you coming with us?'

Clearly he addressed Himself, from the colour that rose in their stagemaster's cheeks.

'Poet,' said Christophe beneath his breath, more unfriendly than teasing. 'Is that a pet-name, lovie?'

They looked like a trio — Livilla in a fur coat that cost far more than any mask or columbine could afford. Her dangerous beau, flicking a fancy fob watch open and closed, like he couldn't be bothered to wait even a minute more than he had to. Himself — *Poet* — impeccably attired in his suit and top hat, leaning towards the two as if pulled into orbit around them, like the moon around the world. He looked at Garnet like he wanted to stab him, or kiss him.

If he chose these friends over the theatricals, Evie had no doubt that someone would get stabbed, and her bet was on Ruby-red or Christophe to wield the weapon.

'I have my company,' Himself said finally. 'Things to do. Stay brilliant.' It was a choice, and a dismissal.

Garnet's face looked perfectly blank, as if no one had ever said 'no' to him before.

Livilla blew kisses before she left on Garnet's arm, and Ruby-red blew more back, as if they were the best of friends.

'She could do better,' Ruby-red said in a mutter, as the company surged away along the street in search of a nox-bar willing to serve cocktails and oysters to this many people at once. 'Did you see his sleeves? Disgraceful.'

'I liked his shoes,' said Christophe. 'And his shoulders,' he added with a half-hearted leer.

'You're a pack of gossipy old cats,' said Himself, but he was smiling. 'First round is on me.'

The company cheered.

8

CONSUALIA (A FESTIVAL OF GRAIN, CHARIOT-RACES & STOLEN WIVES)

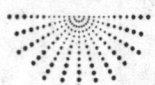

ONE DAY BEFORE THE IDES OF SATURNALIS

DAYLIGHT

*E*vie awoke in Sunshine's bed again the next morning, earlier than anyone else. Her lips were kiss-bruised, and her head ached from too many oysters doused in gin and bitters, followed by drinks that had no connection to oysters at all.

She remembered Christophe and Zephyr resolving their recent spat, and then flirting with other people all nox to prove how uninterested they were in each other.

The theatre was closed; the day before a new season began was considered unofficially *nefas* (unlucky), and the schedule kept clear, unless extra emergency rehearsals were required.

'Last stagemaster to make us work the day before a Saturnalia revue was horribly murdered,' Christophe reminded them all during the drunken oyster breakfast.

'Himself wouldn't dare,' laughed Ruby-red.

Evie had wondered at the time, what did Himself do with a day to... well, a day to himself?

This was her chance to find out. She rose from Sunshine's warm, comfortable bed, dressed herself neatly in a long tunic that disguised her culottes (she could be discreet sometimes), and followed him.

Himself had not slept at the boarding house, which was hardly a surprise by now. Evie found him at the theatre, holed up with paperwork in his dusty studio, above the box office. When he emerged, he wore a muted version of his usual flashy outfit. The jacket was dusty at the sleeves and the waistcoat crumpled as if someone had sat on it deliberately. He had a flat cap covering his hair instead of a fine top hat.

He looked perfectly ordinary.

Evie considered trailing him around in secret, but from what she knew of Himself, he valued honesty. She stepped out from the side-street and nodded to him.

The stagemaster blinked and stared at her through his spectacles as if, for a moment, he had forgotten who she was. 'I don't actually want you to rewrite my saints-and-angel,' he said abruptly.

'That's all right,' said Evie. 'I don't want to either. Especially the literal day before you go before an audience, which is arrant nonsense. I'd like to interview you, if you have the time.'

'For your newspaper story,' he said as if he didn't quite believe she was writing one.

'You're an anomaly in the theatre world. The Orphan Princel — a stage brat who rose from the chorus of the musette to run his own theatre before he turned twenty. My Laudinon newspaper will eat it up with a spoon — and it will be syndicated here in Aufleur too.'

Himself narrowed his eyes at her and she was surprised all over again at how young he looked out of his element. When he commanded the rehearsals, he was a steady presence of confidence and artifice.

There were times when he seemed weary-old, and you'd never believe he was a similar age to Christophe and Ruby-Red. Other times he seemed far younger than the rest of them.

'Come along, then,' Himself said sharply, tugging down his cap. 'I have rounds to make. Keep me company, and I'll answer your questions. If they're interesting enough.'

'How long have you managed the Vittorina Royale?' Evie asked, hastening her step to keep up as he strode down the stairs and out into the street, long legged creature that he was.

'That wasn't an interesting one,' Himself declared. 'Do better.'

THEY VISITED three theatres in as many hours. Himself didn't bother to explain, but Evie figured out what he was up to soon enough.

These were preview matinees — afternoon shows in the rolling musette style, one act after another, that audiences could view for a few centimes. Most were young people after a cheap date, huddling and giggling together in the stalls.

It was nearly Saturnalia, and the Vittorina Royale wasn't the only theatre launching their holiday season this week.

Harlequino and his columbines; monsters and stellars; saints and angels, all spun across the musette stages of the city.

Himself stuck his hands in his pockets as if he'd rather be

anywhere but here, and glowered at every stage. Evie spent more time observing him than the performances.

The Argentia was different, if only because there were more seats available this late in the day. Himself ushered Evie directly to one, making sure she was comfortable on the plush, faded velvet.

'We might be here a while,' he confided.

'Looking for something in particular?'

He gave her a bright grin. 'Wouldn't you like to know?'

'I know you're not combing for ideas,' she muttered. 'Because your show is done, and making changes at this late stage is...'

'I like the phrase *arrant nonsense*. We should use it more often, make it a thing.'

'It's already a thing! It's not a made up phrase, like...'

'The cat's meow?' Himself said slyly.

'The duck's quack,' she countered.

'Hush,' Himself said as the lanterns dimmed around them. 'I've heard this show is the rat's pyjamas.'

Evie snickered into silence.

THE SHOW WAS NOT the rat's pyjamas. It wasn't even the bee's knees.

Half a knee, perhaps, Evie conceded, as their saints-and-angel was a cut above, and they had a half decent harlequinade, though their columbines were feeble.

'Better be careful they don't lure Ruby-red and your lot over here with the promise of better pay and shiny trinkets,' she whispered to Himself. 'They need new blood to liven up their lacklustre first line.'

'They can't have mine,' Himself whispered back. 'We're

haemorrhaging tumblers as it is, three of them have cart-wheeled off to pastures new in the last market-nine. I'm down to understudies.'

When the saints-and-angel gave way to a good old-fashioned cabaret of monsters, Himself leaned forward, more attentive than before. He was here for this.

'You're not looking to steal performers this close to the season?' Evie whispered.

'Of course not. But I won't have time to go headhunting once we're doing four hours of show a day. I'll snatch those kids up for a song in the new year. Make a note. That short one.'

Evie was not taking notes for him. She frowned at the lamb that Himself had indicated. 'He can't sing or dance.'

'That's not the talent I'm looking for.'

One of the children was brighter and better than the others: dark brown beneath a paper mask of a tabby cat, she held herself like a queen, and hit the notes harder and better than the rest of them.

'Find out her name,' Himself ordered with a flick of his hand.

Evie rolled her eyes at him. 'I'm not your secretary.' But she stole a programme for him on their way out, so he could look the tabby cat's name up for himself.

AT THE BAR AFTERWARDS — rolls and ciocolata made a better breakfast than oysters, though Evie was craving coronets and there were none to be had — Himself admitted that he was indeed looking to recruit child performers.

'Lambs are better to work with than adults. Give them square meals and a roof over their heads: they'll learn any

60

words you ask, and hardly any of them steal each other's boyfriends.'

'Does your show even have room for a cabaret of monsters?' Evie asked with her mouth full of soft bread.

'We have to keep moving and changing,' said Himself, waving his cup so expressively that he lost half the ciocolata out of it. 'The show can't stay still. Audiences won't come back in Aphrodal to see the same song and dance numbers they adored in Saturnalis.'

'Will Livilla be part of your show in Aphrodal?' Evie asked lightly. 'Or is she a Saturnalia novelty?'

Himself gave her a dirty look. 'That's not an interesting question,' he warned, but shifted uncomfortably in his chair.

'I've got a good one,' went on Evie. 'Who's Garnet, and exactly what power does he have over both of you?'

Himself set down his cup. He looked altogether less friendly now. 'Are you interested in the theatre at all?'

'I'm more interested in you.'

'Sweet,' he drawled. 'But you're not my type.'

'Nor you mine,' Evie shot back. 'I'm interested in people. Human interest. Social movements. Theatre is the centre of everything in Aufleur, but it's not because of the shows.'

'What do you think it is about, then?'

'Fantasy. Giving the audience something larger than themselves. Watching the saints-and-angel at Saturnalia is probably the most religious experience on offer in this city.'

'You're joking. We have festivals and rituals every day. Where have you been?'

Shut up in a boarding house with your friends and too much gin, she wanted to say.

What she did say was: 'Ritual is routine. Theatre holds the possibility of surprise.'

'That's true enough. Is that what's wrong with —'

'I'm not telling you what's wrong with your saints-and-angel play,' she snapped, catching the disapproving glare of other patrons in the bar. Evidently this was the time of day when everyone in the vicinity was hungover, and loud voices were not encouraged.

Himself shrugged helplessly to the other patrons. 'She's not from around here. Don't mind her.' He leaned in. 'What's wrong with my play?'

Evie sighed. 'I know you don't need me to tell you.'

Himself regarded her with his sharp, thoughtful gaze. 'You couldn't care less about scribbling stories about glamorous reprobates who sing for their supper. I don't think you're a newspaper-demme at all.'

'Of course I am.'

'It's what you do, but it's not why you're here. Tell me a truth or I won't help you a lick, and neither will anyone who works for me.'

'If you're right about me, that's no threat at all,' she shot back, and then sighed. She could give him a partial truth, at least. See what came of it. 'I'm looking for someone. A person who disappeared long ago. I am in Aufleur as a writer, but... I'm looking, as well.'

Himself stilled at her words, humour leeching out of his eyes. When he wasn't animated and laughing, he was quite unpleasant to look at, as if there was no one behind his face. 'You lost them in Aufleur?'

'I think Aufleur was the likeliest destination.'

'And you think they — ?'

'She. My sister.'

'You think she fell to the bohemians?'

'Or the wolves,' Evie said quietly.

There was pain now, just for a moment on his face. 'I can't help you with that. You know I can't.'

'Does he make people disappear, your man Garnet?'

'He's not my man.' That came out fast, like it was the most

truthful thing he'd said to her all day. Like it was a truth he needed to believe.

Evie mopped up the last of her ciocolata with a torn piece of roll. 'We're done here.'

THEY WALKED in silence back to the Vittorina Royale. Garnet waited for Himself at the stage door, fuming like he'd never been made to wait for anything his whole life.

'We need to talk,' he rapped out as Himself and Evie approached. 'About Livilla.'

'Inside, if you please,' said Himself, with more deference than he usually offered anyone else around his theatre. He doffed his cap to Evie. 'There's a cast party at the Dapper, after sundown.'

Evie raised an eyebrow at him. 'Aren't cast parties saved for *after* the season closes?'

'It's Saturnalia,' said Himself with a hint of mockery. 'Everything's upside down and topsy-turvy.'

'And any excuse for a party,' said Evie.

'Any,' agreed Himself. 'Excuse. For a party.' He unlocked the door and waved Garnet ahead of him into the theatre.

Evie didn't hear him latch it on the other side, though.

And that was almost an invitation.

SHE WAITED a few minutes and then crept inside after the two men. She didn't dare risk the creaky staircase, but she didn't need to — everyone knew that if you sat in the box office, you could hear anything from Himself's study above. Ruby-red had told her tales of the last stagemaster, who would deliberately call the prettiest columbines and songbirds up there to 'earn their billing' when his pregnant mistress, their former stellar, was on box office duty.

'Nasty old goat liked everyone to know how expendable they were. Glad he came to a bad end.'

Evie hoped Garnet and Poet wouldn't pick up her presence, even with her heart thudding way too hard in her ears.

She had to hope the acoustics of the box office only went one way.

'Are you kidding me?' Himself snapped. 'Are you really this selfish?'

'I don't care about the two of you playing at theatre,' said Garnet, his voice relaxing into a country accent.

'Oh, thank you very much.'

'Poet, this isn't about that.'

'Isn't it?'

'Livilla's been different lately. Have you not noticed?'

'She needed something that wasn't the nox or the court or the war, Garnet. She needed one fucking thing in her life that doesn't revolve around you.'

'You dare…'

'This is my theatre,' said Himself, high and cold. 'You are not Power and Majesty here.'

'Fix Livilla,' Garnet snarled. 'The sky almost killed her the other nox because she was distracted. She hasn't fought so badly since she was new meat. Make her give up this stellar nonsense. Or I will burn your precious theatre to the ground.'

Evie heard a crash and a bang from above. She froze for an instant, not sure if she should cut and run or wait and pretend she was meant to be here.

A streak of gold and spots bounded down the stairs. She sucked in a breath as it stopped for a moment — *gattopardo*, a proud and dangerous big cat, she'd only seen one in the zoo before — and gazed at her with eyes like jewels.

Garnet was not a wolf.

The gattopardo swished its tail and then leaped from the steps to the foyer, and nudged its way through to the main theatre, heading for that back door.

Evie let out her breath, and waited for him to be gone.

This was going to be harder than she had thought.

9

ONE NOX BEFORE THE
IDES OF SATURNALIS

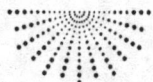

DUSK

*E*vie returned to the boarding house, her thoughts a confused jumble of insights about the man who was variously called the Orphan Princel, the stagemaster, Himself and... Poet?

She had to stop letting these people tangle her further into their lives. She had one task here in Aufleur. Terrifying as he was, Garnet was her mission, not the theatricals.

When she let herself into her room, Evie found the wolves waiting for her.

They splayed out on her bed, tongues lolling, eyes lidded and heavy. Two of them: slender and deadly. The second the door snapped shut behind her, they came alert, blazing gold irises holding her in place.

'There's no need for games,' Evie said, tired and wanting to take her shoes off. 'I know who you are.'

Livilla's different, Garnet had said. Different how? If *wolf*

66

and *gattopardo* and *bat* were normal, then… what did different mean?

The wolves fell into each other; became one larger wolf, all haunch and hackle. Her lip curled up into a growl that reverberated across the antique floorboards.

Evie had faced down worse than this. She used to cover debutante balls back in Laudinon. The aunts at those things were the most vicious creatures she had ever encountered.

She stepped further into the room. 'There's no need to hide,' she said.

The wolf shifted into bare, human flesh. Livilla's perfect face still wore exquisite cosmetick, framed by her black, bobbed hair. Her clothes did not come with the change, but the lip-paint did. How did that even work?

Livilla made no move to dress herself, though it was freezing in here. It might be nearly noon, but Evie could feel the Saturnalis chill through her boots and the tweed coat that wasn't quite enough to keep winter at bay.

Livilla's naked belly was unmarked. There was no sign of the wounds that had almost killed her so very recently. Had they almost killed her? Or was this some wolf-and-flapper game that Evie wasn't in on?

'What happened to you?' Evie blurted.

Livilla gave a twisted smile, creasing her bright red lip-paint. 'That's a long story.'

'I'd like to hear it.'

'Oh, no. You won't see my dirty laundry scattered over the Aufleur Gazette, or whatever muckraking rag you write for.'

'All the newspapers,' admitted Evie. 'Evander X stories are syndicated across more than a dozen papers across Ammoria, Inglirra and beyond. Poet made you a stellar, but I… could make you famous.'

Evie wasn't making the promise because she intended to

keep it — though she could, it would be great fun. But she was more interested in how Livilla reacted to the promise of fame and fortune.

Livilla laughed, hard as glass. 'The demme who turned into wolves,' she quipped. 'I'm not a novelty act for your amusement, Inglirra.'

'I never said you were.' Evie took a step closer to the naked woman. Livilla was spectacular with her clothes off, all curves and angles. She should be painted with a vase and a flower crown. She should hang on the walls of a museion.

She could eat Evie alive.

'What are you?' Evie asked softly.

Livilla took a step of her own, closer. 'What are you?' she countered. 'I see you, cuddling up to Kip and Ruby-red's crowd like they're your new best friends. But there's something off about you. I know how people work, and you're...' She narrowed her eyes.

'An outsider?'

'A liar. Takes one to know one.' Livilla took another step closer, her bare breasts almost brushing the lapels of Evie's embroidered coat. 'What are you looking for, here in Aufleur?'

Evie considered telling Livilla the same story she had left with Himself, the thread she cast at him in the hope it would get back to Garnet. It was too late to make a decision about that now, because Livilla was kissing her. She laid her arms in a lazy sprawl around Evie's shoulders and leaned in, her bright carmine mouth opening, tasting.

Evie kissed back. She had no defence against a beautiful woman in her arms. They necked slowly, bodies warm against each other — honestly, why wasn't Livilla cold?

Only a scrape of teeth made Evie pull back. She had heard many rumours about the secret people of Aufleur, the ones who changed into lions and wolves (and gattopardo, it seemed). One of those rumours was that they drank blood...

'I lost someone,' Evie blurted, kiss-drunk and starting to panic as the very calm Livilla leaned back to observe her. 'I think she came here, to Aufleur.'

'Thousands of people come here,' said Livilla. 'It's a famous city of prosperity and wonder. People get lost on the streets of Aufleur every day.' She licked her lips very deliberately as if to imply she was the reason they got lost. 'Lover?'

'Sister,' Evie admitted.

Livilla's expression did not change. 'How long ago?'

'Ten years.'

'Oh sweetie. What took you so long?'

'I was a child,' Evie said flatly. 'We were both children. She was supposed to be travelling with an aunt.'

'So unreliable, aunts.'

'Neither of them were ever heard of again.'

'But you think your sister came here?'

'I had a postcard a year ago,' Evie insisted. 'Hardly anything at all, a picture of the Vittorina Royale and unsigned, but I know it was from her. She wanted me to know she was alive, that she made it out of whatever took her from us. She always wanted to be an actress when we were children — Mama would never have allowed that. I thought this was a place to start, at least.' Did she sound desperate enough? Hopeless enough?

Livilla moved away, all business, She picked up a fallen silk robe from Evie's bed which hadn't been there this morning — another of Ruby-red's glamorous collection which were flung all around the boarding house like a cat shedding fur. 'I wouldn't get my hopes up, if I were you,' Livilla remarked. 'What was her name, this sister?'

'Kennalise,' said Evie. 'But we called her Kelpie.'

She was watching for it, or she would never have seen the brief second in which Livilla froze. The story took hold.

'Never heard of her,' Livilla said airily, lying through her teeth. 'So many theatres across Ammoria, we're a decadent sort of place. If you can't find her in the big city, try a coastal town or two. Small communities, cheaper tickets. That's where the dregs wash up.'

'I'll keep that in mind,' said Evie, and wiped Livilla's lip-paint from her own mouth.

LIVILLA'S BETRAYAL WAS EFFICIENT. Two hours later, Evie was kidnapped.

First, she typed up the latest frivolous column to drop in to Jardin Falcone's paper when she had a minute, capturing the atmosphere of the matinees she had endured with Himself all day, with a few gossipy hints about the audience, and the anticipation of the city's Saturnalia theatre season.

She never got a chance to file the story. The moment she set foot outside her door in search of tea and company, she was attacked.

They slammed into her from behind, shoving a sack over her head and holding her arms. Evie forced herself to only struggle a little, then fell limp as they carried her down the stairs out of the boarding house.

'I don't like this,' muttered the voice of a youth.

'Aye, and we know that well enough,' shot back an older man, with an accent from Evie's side of the Orcadian Strait. 'The rest of us are clearly having a whale of a time.'

'Don't talk,' said a woman in a low, serious voice. 'You'll give too much away.'

Evie let out an 'oof' as she was tipped into a handcart of some kind, and felt the ground rattling behind her. She stayed limp, doing her best to pretend she was a sack of potatoes.

She had places to be.

They travelled for a while, sometimes bumping her over a surface not meant for a hand-cart, then rattling along a much smoother path. It was colder now, and damp. Even through the blindfold she could tell it was darker than before.

Here was one story she had heard about the sinister creatures who made Aufleur more dangerous than any other city: they lived underground.

Was she finally about to discover the truth behind the fairy tale?

The cart tipped, and Evie hit the hard ground. She felt grit under her palms, and a sticky dampness to the paving stones. Sturdy fingers worked into the knots behind her scalp, releasing the blindfold.

Evie sat up, hanging on to what was left of her dignity. Two men in thick brown cloaks loomed over her: one short, craggy and threatening; the other young and pretty enough to dance alongside Christophe on stage.

'Why am I here?' she asked, keeping things polite for now. There would be time enough to stick a hatpin into one of them and run like hells; she always had a pin or two on her person for such an occasion, though she rarely bothered with hats.

'You've been askin' too many questions, so you have,' said the shorter one in a voice more Islandser than Inglirran, but familiar all the same.

Evie raised her eyebrows. 'You're a long way from home, son. And asking questions is *literally* the job of a newspaper-demme. Do you kidnap us by the dozen and keep us locked up in one of your…' She glanced around the area which looked like some grim underground warehouse without a barrel of imperium or crate of apples to be seen. 'I suppose dungeon is the word I'm looking for.'

Someone had gone to a lot of trouble to make this dump look grand. Lanterns hung from a balconied roof above a boxy warehouse built into the round walls. Swords and daggers were pinned up and down on every surface, always in pairs. A swish of red satin hung in front of the doors. Iron hooks ran along a lower archway, with clothes draped from them: fine, theatrical clothes, all silks and leather.

A fancy dungeon with pretentions of grandeur, but a dungeon nevertheless. It smelled like dead air and rodents.

'Like to talk, don't you,' the Islandser marvelled. 'Are you not worried what we might do to you?'

'Oh,' said Evie, giving him a chilly look. 'I don't imagine you're in charge.'

'I have a question,' said a voice from directly behind her. It was a demme, the same demoiselle who had spoken when Evie was being trundled around like baggage.

Evie stayed very still.

The demme moved into sight, walking slowly to stand beside her companions. She wore a brown cloak too, with a rough outfit of trews and shirt beneath.

Finally, another demme in this city willing to wear trousers. 'What's your question?' Evie asked, though she had a feeling she had already guessed the substance of it.

'Who the hell are you?' snarled the demme, hand hovering over her belt as if she expected to find a dagger waiting for her to grasp. '*I'm* Kelpie, it's not short for anything, and *you are not my sister.*'

This, of course, was the problem with being a professional liar. Sooner or later, the stories caught up with you.

'No,' said Evie calmly, allowing her gaze to hold Kelpie's. 'I'm not your sister.'

'Then why would you say —'

'Peace, Kelpie,' said the Islandser, their leader. 'Garnet said naught of an interrogation.'

'Do you do everything Garnet says?' Evie asked.

None of them replied to that, but their expressions were everything.

They were guards of some kind, these three; bodyguards, perhaps? Why did a man who could turn into a beast require bodyguards? They held themselves as if their entire function was to stand between a person with a weapon and a person who paid them.

Not one of them carried a weapon.

'Why are there so many swords on the walls, and none in your belts?' Evie asked aloud.

'Mind your own business,' said the Islandser gruffly. Clearly this was a sore point.

Knowing where to dig at sore points was a skill that Evie prided herself upon, and one which often reaped better rewards than the lying. 'Are *they* your swords?'

'Shut your face.'

Laughter echoed through the dank cavern. Human laughter, though the figure who leaped on to the railing of the balcony and prowled across its edge was gattopardo, entirely.

The big cat made a leap to the stairs and shaped himself human as he walked. Garnet, naked and brazen as an actor backstage, reached out and took a silk kimono from the hooks as he reached the floor, wrapping his body. 'Answer the demoiselle's question, Macready,' he said in a tone that could only be a threat. 'Are they your swords?'

'No, my Majesty,' said the Islandser, his eyes on the ground. His hand twitched and Evie saw for the first time that it had been mutilated; his ring finger was missing and there was an ugly twist of pink scarring left behind that twisted his entire hand.

'Crane, are they your swords?'

'No, my Power,' said the younger man, also staring at the ground.

Evie looked from one to the other, her gaze finally settling back on Kelpie.

'I want to know why she said she was my *sister*,' Kelpie said angrily. Unlike the others, she did not treat Garnet as if he were about to whip her.

Garnet raised his eyebrows. 'Well, muckraker? Is Kelpie remotely important to the story you spun around us?'

'No,' said Evie honestly. She gave Kelpie a half-shrug. 'I wanted to catch his attention. I'd apologise but you just hit me over the head and kidnapped me, so I'm not feeling overly friendly. Maybe in a year or two we can laugh about it over drinks.' She ignored the furious demme, turning back to Garnet. 'You'll want the rest of our conversation to be private.'

He prowled around her, keeping his distance as he circled her. Clearly he was used to having these cloaked servants stand between himself any anyone he didn't trust, or he wouldn't come so close. '*Will* I want that?'

The best thing about eavesdropping was that you found out people's hidden weaknesses... and no one ever thought it happened to them. 'There's something wrong with Livilla,' Evie told him.

Garnet went very still, his face hard as a statue. 'What have you heard?'

'Nothing you'll want others to know about.'

He hesitated only a moment, and then dismissed the brown-cloaks with a wave. 'Get out.'

'Majesty,' said the Islandser Macready. 'How can we protect you —'

'That's a good question,' Garnet smirked, all his attention on Evie. 'How can you protect me? What exactly is the point of Sentinels without their shiny swords? I thank you for bringing me this baggage and now you will *leave me alone*.'

The three of them left, conditioned to obey.

'My hands are still tied,' Evie told her captor.

'I'm aware,' said Garnet. 'Were you expecting to be treated kindly?'

'Sadly for you,' said Evie. 'I keep my tongue in my wrists. I can't tell you anything while I'm bound.'

Her wit amused rather than angered him. With all the confidence of a man who could shape into a big cat and maul her at a moment's notice, Garnet walked behind her and untied the ropes. 'Glass of wine? Honey cake?'

'Thank you,' said Evie. 'I'm thoroughly refreshed. I was splashed by a puddle or two when your friends were trundling me along in their handcart. That should see me through to breakfast.'

Garnet's eyes narrowed. 'Tell me about Livilla.'

'Don't you want to know how I found you?' Evie asked. 'Don't you want to know how I know what you are?'

Clearly that enraged him, though he remained calm and polite. Garnet's fury was all in his eyes. 'No one knows what I am.'

'No curiosity at all? Really. Your friend Poet was right — people never ask interesting questions.'

Garnet extended a hand to help her to her feet. His skin was warm to the touch, too warm, as if he ran a fever. 'Livilla has been acting differently ever since she agreed to take part in Poet's theatre bullshit. Ever since you came to this city. Coincidence?'

Evie shrugged. She might not be a mask or a tumbler, but she knew how to use artifice to cover her real intentions. She'd been doing it all her life. 'Coincidence. I never met Livilla until after she was introduced to all the fancy patrons of the theatre. If you're right and she's changed somehow… it was before then.'

'How do you know that?'

'Ruby-red says Livilla can't sing that well. This Livilla, the one you're so worried about, she sings like an angel. Like a saint playing an angel, or an angel playing a saint.'

'Livilla can sing,' said Garnet, looking almost offended on the demme's behalf. 'She has a pretty voice.'

'Does she have a magnificent voice, a trained voice, a voice that could shatter glass and win the hearts of heroes and fill a theatre full of posh nobs with money to burn?' Evie challenged him.

Garnet hesitated. 'I don't…'

'I knew I was better at asking questions than you were.' Evie moved away from him, meandering around the great empty space like a tourist taking in the sights. She stopped to peer at the costumes hung on hooks. She paused by the staircase as if she might head upstairs and nose around. She wandered around until she was directly beneath the wide array of swords and daggers, pinned to the wall in pairs. 'These are pretty. Are they trophies?'

'Something like that,' said Garnet. 'Are you suggesting that Livilla is… possessed in some way? That someone replaced her? Someone with a show-stopping voice.'

'Am I suggesting that?' Evie asked in return. 'How should I know what's even possible around here? I'm not the one living in a dark underground world of fairy tales.' She reached up thoughtfully and tapped the tip of one of the daggers with her finger. It was sharp.

'Don't touch those,' said Garnet. 'What do you mean, fairy tales?'

'That's how I found you,' said Evie. 'Talk about questions unasked. You haven't even wondered how I know you can shape yourself into animals. Gattopardo.'

'I assume you are not of the daylight,' he said in a crisp voice. 'There are other cities, other Courts. You belong to one of them. Clearly.'

'Not one of the daylight. I don't know what you even mean by that,' said Evie. 'I'm practically nocturnal these days. As for Courts... there are no Courts in Laudinon except that which our ruling Duke commands, and it's mostly stuffy old gentlemen eating big meals and challenging each other to chess games.'

'But,' said Garnet, and then he stopped. 'You found me.'

'I'm good at finding things,' said Evie. 'Mostly, I follow stories. Once you know what to look for, there are a lot of clues to be found in Ammorian folklore. Stories for children about owls turning into women, princes becoming ponies. Pretty men drinking blood. Invisible swords. That sort of thing.' She reached out and tapped the point of another dagger. This one fell into her hand too deep; it should have drawn blood. She felt nothing but a light buzz against her skin, like the soft flutter of a bee passing by. 'Interesting.'

'There are no stories about us,' said Garnet scornfully. 'About the old war, perhaps. But not any more. *No one knows.*'

'And yet, I found you,' said Evie. 'All I had to do was follow the right story, plant the right seed. Here I am, in a secret underground city that shouldn't exist.' She gave her arms a bit of a flourish. 'I'm very good at what I do.'

'Writing stories,' Garnet scoffed. 'Trashy tales for sex-starved readers. Profiles of ordinary, boring daylight people with humdrum lives.'

Evie tapped her fingers thoughtfully against the dagger on the wall, the one nearest to her, its hilt wrapped in blue leather. The hilt was solid enough but the blade, the blade was as insubstantial as air. She'd never seen anything like it.

Someone had once told her a story about a knife like this.

'Selling stories pays the bills,' she informed her kidnapper. 'But it's not actually what I do. In the vocational sense.'

'What's that supposed to mean?' Garnet demanded, his voice rising. 'Step away from that wall.'

Evie turned to face him, smiling a wide and welcoming smile. Her best smile. 'It's important to love your work,' she told him, and her hand moved fast. She seized the impossible knife, flipped it in her hand and threw it with a speed and strength that the man never saw coming.

Garnet's eyes widened as the knife drove into his throat, and he fell to the ground in a crumpled heap of limbs and silk kimono.

10

LIVILLA

BEFORE SATURNALIS

NOX

*W*hen I first set foot in the Vittorina Royale all those years ago, it was impossibly grand. The only theatre I'd known before that was our old Mermaid, held together with bobby pins and hope. The Vittorina Royale in the Big City of Aufleur had gilded paint and crowned panels in the ceiling, a long sweep of red velvet curtain. The stage was so wide you could run from one side to the other, or do three backflips with room for more.

It has been more than a decade since I set foot in this place. Ashiol and Mars attend the plays sometimes, to tease Poet with their presence, but I could never bring myself to cross back into this world of greasepaint and centime-opera.

I barely cared when Poet took the theatre for himself. That was the first Saturnalia after Garnet became Power and Majesty; Lysandor and Celeste fled the city to escape his jealous cruelty. It was all blood and chaos; is it any wonder that it took a while to notice Poet with his daylight schemes?

Somehow our urchin brat with the big eyes transformed himself into a seigneur, all velvet suits and dapper manners. I don't know where he got the money from or where the old goat of a stagemaster went... but I did see the change in Poet, the swagger and the poise. The fine coats and top hat he affected to wear.

Part of me feared that if I set foot in the Vittorina Royale again, the costume I wore as Wolf Lord Livilla would fall away, leaving me as skinny, knock-kneed Liv in her cheap leather mask. A demme without a place in the world.

I know it can't be as beautiful as I remember.

That was five years ago; Poet is a man now. He fights the sky with us every nox, a battle-hardened Lord of Rats. The rest of the time... he plays as being stagemaster at the Vittorina Royale. He has found a place for himself. He has a foot in both worlds and he makes it work in a way none of the rest of us have ever managed.

I can do this now.

I am a *wolf*.

I let him cut my hair. My neck is cold.

We step inside and the theatre is... beautiful. Brighter and grander than in my memory, if that's even possible. I remember what it was like to belong here, and it breaks my heart.

'What exactly is the point of this?' I ask Poet.

He smirks at me from behind those spectacles that conceal so much, and guides me up to the stage. 'I'm going to make you a stellar.'

'You realise my greatest talents are fighting the sky and transforming into wolves?' I have no illusions that I could make it as a songbird now any more than I could back then. Am I expected to dance? Tumble? He'd better have a mask that can fit me.

'Believe me,' Poet says in a mock-pout, 'I've considered it. I just don't think we could explain the special effects.'

'I shouldn't be here.' I must be such a fool. *I let him cut my hair.*

Poet's eyes are fierce and shining. 'You're the fucking Lord of Wolves, Livilla. You're the only warrior of the Creature Court who isn't afraid of our Power and Majesty. You're glorious. I want you on my stage because I'm selfish, because you'll make me look good, and...' He hesitates. 'I don't want you and I to end up hating each other, like Garnet and Tasha... Lysandor... Ashiol.'

Names of our packmates, our family, all gone now but Garnet, and he's not our friend any more. Not since he started to rule us.

'So you thought making me look ridiculous was a good start?' I snipe at him.

'Fighting the sky and turning into wolves aren't your only talents, Liv,' Poet assures me. 'You're also brilliant at wearing clothes dramatically and being mean, both essential skills for the stellar of a fine establishment like this one.'

That makes me laugh, at least. 'Screw you.'

'Not in a million years, my sweet.'

He's waiting for me to sing. I won't. I can't. I'm not a songbird. I never found my place in the theatre — I ran away to become a wolf, instead.

There is a song, something I used to sing to the pack when they were hurt or afraid. I sing it to my courtesi, when they need the comfort of a Lord who loves them. That at least, I can do.

Standing there in my ordinary clothes, with the too-short hair I haven't figured out if I love or hate yet, I start to sing in a voice that's too sweet, too quiet. Maybe Poet will finally realise I'm not good enough, that I have no more business being a stellar of the Vittorina Royale than I had thinking I could be a stagemaster someday.

Thinking I could be Power and Majesty.

I sing for him. I sing my fucking heart out, sing until my chest hurts and my eyes water, and it doesn't matter because I'm untrained, out of practice, not good enough.

I can feel the theatre inside my bones. My face is painted gilt and pearlescent white; if you cut me open right now, I would bleed red velvet. I am the theatre.

I am

Something has

Oh, I see it now. I always thought of the theatre and the Creature Court as separate spaces — the theatre as daylight, and the Court as nox. We fight the sky, and then Poet goes home to his masks and mummers and tumblers and columbines and songbirds…

There's a hole in the ceiling of the Vittorina Royale. I never saw it before I started singing. But the sky… the sky knew it was there. The sky is bleeding into the theatre, into my song, into my veins.

Saturnalia is nearly upon us, the season of topsy-turvy, of men dressed as women and lambs as old men. The noble scions of the Great Families dress as peasants and laugh about it, while insisting the maids and valets prance around in the cast-offs from their masters.

Saturnalia is a festival when the impossible comes true, when the world turns upside down.

I'm singing like a stellar, a voice big enough to bring the house down, and Poet is looking at me like I'm beautiful. Like I'm worth something.

There's something inside my head that wasn't there before, a piece of the sky that tastes like the theatre.

Who are you? I ask my invader.

Oh, dearling, says the bright white light. *I'm the one who's going to make you a stellar. And they will never see you coming.*

11
SEVERAL MARKET-NINES AGO

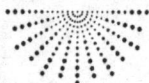

BEFORE EVIE CAME TO AUFLEUR

*E*vanderline Inglirra had often been invited into houses like this: manors and estates more like castles than ordinary homes. Houses full of servants and stray cousins and furniture older than anyone still living.

It never ceased to amaze her, the way toffs were so determined to be waited upon that they invited anyone they wished to do business with into their home, even a snake like her.

This particular manor was on the fancier side of Ammorian country hospitality. The gardens were enormous enough that the driveway could do with its own railway.

From the looks that Evie had received from the maids and the other servants, it was the first time any woman had ever dared wear trousers in this house. She had known that before she accepted the invitation, but she found it interesting to see how people reacted to such a slight challenge to the code of conventional behaviour.

If they clutched their pearls at the sight of her legs outlined in soft linen, they likely had no stomach for her line of work, and even less stomach for paying a woman to perform such work.

These were the clients to watch; they'd hire you all the same, but stiff you on the deal later.

When the Dowager Baronnille Augusta Xandelian finally entered the exquisite drawing room to attend her guest, she did not bat an eyelid at Evie's expertly tailored trews. That was a good sign.

The Dowager Baronnille, daughter of the recently deceased Duc of Aufleur and aunt of the new Duchessa, was a matronly dame in a gown built for comfort rather than fashion. There was more dark than grey in her hair, which she wore in a soft mass on top of her head, all loose curls and pins. She would have been all the mode only a few years ago, before the women of the big cities began to shingle and bob.

Evie had almost refused the invitation. She knew far less about the Great Families of Aufleur than she should, and was concerned at the risks if she failed to grasp the subtle inner threads of this foreign society. She was — however slightly — outside her comfort zone.

Everything she had learned about this woman from afar told her that the Dowager Baronnille Augusta was not a dame who would hire a killer without a very good reason. There was nothing more tantalising to Evie than a question unanswered.

So she was here, a thousand miles from home, sipping tea in a fancy room full of loudly ticking clocks, waiting to find out what made a wealthy twice-widow from a ducal family desperate enough to call upon an assassin.

If she did, would Evie take the job? All excellent questions.

The Dowager Baronnille helped herself to tea without calling for assistance — another mark in her favour, another note that marked her out as more interesting than your standard fancypants dame with more diamonds than sense.

'They call you the Storyteller,' the Dowager Baronnille said calmly, settling in a violet chair opposite Evie's, which was sea-green.

'Indeed they do,' said Evie.

Augusta's eyes were wise and knowing. 'It's not only because of your cover as a newspaper-demme, is it? But that's what you want people to think.'

'You're people,' said Evie with a smirk. 'It's what I want you to think.'

'They say you don't just — remove people,' said Augusta. 'You *disappear* them. They also say that… you could kill a ghost. A witch. A whisper of a person who barely has a foot in the real world.'

'I've done all those things,' said Evie. 'I'm very good.'

'That's exactly what I need,' said Augusta. Her face looked well and truly haunted now. 'Have you heard stories about Aufleur?'

'Everyone's heard stories about Aufleur,' said Evie. Blood and beasts and secrets, a war that rained down from the sky and then disappeared. 'If you talk to someone who lives there, it sounds like a lovely place to be. Honey cakes and ribbons.'

Augusta gave a hollow laugh. 'I need someone who can look past the honey cakes and ribbons,' she said. 'Someone who can dig into where the monsters live, beneath the surface of the city.'

'Ah,' said Evie, trying not to look too excited. 'That sounds like something of interest to a Storyteller. What do you have against monsters?'

'One of them destroyed my son,' said Augusta.

There was the rub. Most dames who hired an assassin wanted to rid themselves of a husband. But the Dowager

Baronnille Augusta Xandelian had lost both her husbands already, under perfectly unsuspicious circumstances.

She had five sons, according to Evie's research, and a young scrap of a daughter who behaved every bit as though she was a sixth. They were all heirs to the duchy until the new Duchessa had her own babies, but Evie would not have been invited openly to this house if the Dowager Baronnille plotted genuine treason.

The clocks on every surface in the lovely room all ticked louder, as if Evie was on to something.

'I passed your sons as I came up the driveway,' Evie said honestly. 'An amiable lot, by the look of them, swinging lawn tennis racquets and riding horses. Which of them do you consider to have been destroyed?'

'My eldest,' said Augusta gravely. 'Ashiol.'

'Oh, the one in the fine coat who needs a haircut,' said Evie. It was a guess, but there was quite an age gap between the eldest and second eldest of Augusta's sons, so hardly a stab in the dark. 'He glowered at me on my way in.'

'He's doing better,' Augusta admitted. 'But that city nearly killed him. And now… our family summons him back to support his cousin, and I can't let him go. Not if the monster is still there, waiting for him.'

'I'm good with monsters,' said Evie. 'But I'll need every thread you can give me. Every rumour. Every word. Killing fairy tales is more difficult than husbands. It requires a lot of groundwork.'

'I have nothing solid,' the Dowager Baronnille admitted. 'Ashiol never spoke about his time in Aufleur. I know he fell in with a bad crowd, full of secrets and strangeness. Criminals. Drug addicts. He was addled and broken, when he was brought home to me. He made it through withdrawal. Suicide attempts. He still drinks too much. I — it felt at times as if my son did not return at all, only a shade of the boy I knew.'

'There are many potions and powders that can do that to a man,' said Evie. This wouldn't be the first drug ring she had hunted, if that was what the lady wanted of her.

'It was more than that,' said Augusta Xandelian, so quietly that the words almost stayed within her mouth. 'There was — I should show you rather than tell you. This is why, when I began to research ways to rid myself of my son's tormentor, your reputation caught my eye. This is why I need a Story-teller, not a knife or a sword.'

She lifted a brown leather journal from the side table where her abandoned cup of tea awaited her. 'His ravings were so strange and yet quite specific, as if a thousand fairy tales filled his head and spilled over. It all — there was a coherence to it that made it feel —' The Dowager Baronnille broke off.

'True,' said Evie.

'True,' Augusta agreed. She handed over the book.

Evie flipped through it. Words and sentence fragments, underlined here and there, making little sense.

Animor. Creature King. Chimaera. Lords and Court. Sentinel. The sky is falling. The city is burning. The Arches. The Haymar-ket. The Museion. Skysilver.

There were sketches, too, in the Dowager Baronnille's hand, presumably to pass the time as she sat by her son's bedside and waited to see if he would live.

Black cats. Rats. Spotted gattopardo. Owls. Wolves, the Ammorian type of wolf that was narrower and shaggier than those of the Inglirran forests. The streets of Aufleur, twisted and different. Swords and roses, swords and roses, swords and…

'How will I find my mark?' asked Evie, closing the journal with a snap. This, she could work with.

'I know a handful of names,' Augusta said. 'They're written there, in the book. Livilla. Mars. Saturn. Tasha. Poet. A theatre, the Vittorina Royale. As for the monster at the heart of it all — He grew up here, on this estate. His name was Garnet. I don't know what he calls himself now. When my son suffers the most, in his dreams, that is the name he screams.'

'Garnet,' Evie repeated.

'I need him gone from Aufleur, never to return,' said Augusta. 'If that means you have to kill him...'

'Well,' said Evie. 'Let's be realistic. Of course that means I have to kill him.'

GARNET BLED red like any other man.

The stories about invisible swords were true. The knife blade that did not even tickle Evie's finger had cut Garnet's throat like it was forged to be the death of him.

He lay on the harsh grey stones, his body fighting for air as his throat bubbled with blood.

Evie leaned in. 'My client sends you greetings from Ashiol Xandelian,' she said politely.

She hated that part of it, an unnecessary flourish, but she took pride in her work and if that means issuing words of vengeance to a person who would shortly hear nothing more, well.

That was why they paid her the big coin.

Garnet's face changed in that instant — not with anger, but fear.

This was why Evie valued words so much. A sentence that could make a dying man even more afraid? That was a power no weapon could match.

She leaned over him, ready to draw the blade away the

second he was dead. She wasn't one for keeping trophies, but this was a dagger she yearned to own, and there was no one to say she could not keep it…

Pain burst into her body from the side, and Evie flew — floated — *slammed* into the wall. Slowly, she spat out a mouthful of blood, and pushed herself up.

Livilla, stellar of the Vittorina Royale, stood between Evie and Garnet, in a glittering gown of beads and feathers. Not the angel costume. This one was all black, with silver threads that danced like fringe around her knees.

'You're ruining my plans,' said the demoiselle who turned into wolves, though she did not look angry. She did not look as if she cared about anything, least of all the dying man on the floor behind her.

'Garnet doesn't think you're yourself,' Evie said quietly, pushing herself to her feet. Her muscles were bruised, and something was torn that made her hip scream at her, but nothing was broken.

She should have paid more attention to Livilla. Evie had used her as a distraction, not thinking it would matter one way or another. It mattered now.

'Garnet,' said Livilla in a mocking voice. 'Who would have thought he was the one to notice? Her lover, Mars — the one who actually loves her, *he* didn't see it. Her courtesi, the young wolf and the raven — *they* didn't see it. Poet, who opened the doors of his theatre to her — who let me inside, *he* still thinks he did her a favour. None of them saw the obvious, except the man who sees everything because he's so damned scared of what he has left to lose.'

'You're not Livilla,' said Evie. 'But you are dangerous.'

'Takes one to know one,' said the creature behind Livilla's eyes.

THE IDES OF SATURNALIS

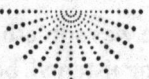

ONE DAY BEFORE SATURNALIA

DAYLIGHT

Evie had seen possession before. She was the Storyteller. Clients rarely paid her fee to kill ordinary humans. She had once slashed the throat of an old man in a haunted house, releasing a dozen or more wraiths that had latched on to his soul. She once murdered a woman who was born with an angel inside her head.

She had defeated devils with a holy blade, and saints with a cursed axe. She was good at her job. Whatever was inside Livilla, it was powerful, and an invisible knife might not be enough to finish her off.

(Evie had not been paid to take out Livilla, and she wasn't a charity foundation.)

'All I need is for him to die,' she said calmly. Garnet still lived. Whatever power turned him into a gattopardo was stringing things out. She could hear the small wet sound of him managing, impossibly, to breathe despite the knife in his throat. 'Then I'll be out of your hair. I don't care what you do to this city. I'll be on the first train out of here.'

Evie didn't usually lie to herself, except when she had to. She didn't realise she was lying until she said the words. But she did care about a piece of this city. She cared about Christophe and Sunshine. Even bitchy Ruby-red with her flouncing and sly looks.

Ruby-red knew there was something wrong with Livilla from the start, and no one listened, because a second columbine hating the stellar, that was the natural order of things.

Livilla stepped closer, eyeing Evie like she was coronets for breakfast. 'I thought I wouldn't need to upgrade,' she said. 'What could be better than wolves and a Saturnalia angel? But you. You're fascinating.'

'I'm nothing special,' said Evie, who had worked hard to become so.

'You look ordinary, but you're a weapon. I wonder if I can turn you into wolves…' She gnashed her teeth briefly and grinned a quirky little grin.

'I'd rather you didn't try to find out,' Evie said quickly.

'You're new in this city,' Livilla mused. 'No one will care if you're different.'

That stung.

'I've done my job,' said Evie. 'It's time for me to go.'

'He's not dead yet,' said Livilla, taking another step forward as if they were going to kiss again, as if that was all this had ever been about: some grand, twisted seduction.

Evie opened her mouth to protest, to say *something*, to talk herself the hells out of this situation, but then her head burned with white light, and her limbs no longer felt like they belonged to her.

She was laughing, and she did not know why. Her whole body shook with helpless sobs of laughter. She tilted back against the wall, watching the world through lidded eyes and swirls of colour.

Livilla — the real Livilla, herself again, hard as nails and brittle as glass — spun around and ran to the fallen figure of Garnet, screaming a word that meant nothing to Evie though she had seen it once, scribbled in a journal of a madman's ravings about this city. 'Sentinels!'

Evie lost time.

～

SHE BLINKED and she was back at the boarding house, watching her friends scurry about, painting cosmetick on their faces and throwing stockings at each other...

'Who are you?' she asked the bright light inside her skull.

'Call me Stellar,' replied the laughing creature. 'Look at you now, Evander X. So many secrets, you don't know which version of you is real.'

'I know who I am,' said Evie, but she couldn't feel angry about it. Couldn't feel much of anything.

'You don't know much,' said the bright light, the stellar inside. 'Let's sing about it.'

'I can't sing,' said Evie, with her own mouth. Christophe and Sunshine stopped in the middle of their flurry, to stare at her.

'A little late for that, sweetheart,' said Sunshine.

Another shuffle of lost time, like leaves in a book.

～

EVIE BLINKED.

Evie was.

Evie was the stellar.

~

SHE WATCHED from backstage as the show went on around her, Himself's show… Poet's show. The first round of the Saturnalia revue. The Vittorina Royale was alive in a way that theatres only were when there was a performance and an audience.

I belong here, Evie thought, surprising herself.

Too late, she realised that it was not her thought.

Sunshine came out of nowhere, dressed in their outfit from one of the skits: a suit that wasn't a suit, half seigneur with cravat, trews and shirt slashed open and sewn down the middle to half of a flapper gown with sequins.

'Subtle,' Evie said through lips that felt numb, in a body no longer wholly her own.

'Shut up, this is theatre, we don't do subtle,' said Sunshine, and kissed her for a moment, cleverly keeping their layers of cosmetick to themselves. 'I don't know how you talked Himself into this,' they added, then whirled away on to the stage before Evie could answer.

What exactly had Evie talked Himself into? She had no idea.

Christophe, bright and colourful as a harlequinus, came breathless off the stage and caught Evie's hand, pulling her with him as he ran back through a mess of half-naked performers to a dressing room.

A room with a star on the door.

'You've barely got your face on,' he chided. 'Where's that demme who was supposed to paint you up?'

'She's busy, I've got this,' said Ruby-red of all people, tugging Evie away from Christophe. 'You're due on stage again in seven, why are you even here?'

'I'll make it,' said Christophe, but he obeyed her quickly and quietly.

There was no arguing back here, no drama. They saved the tears and catfights for rehearsals and breakfasts. For folk who had always seemed so scatty and erratic, the theatricals moved like parts of a well-oiled clockwork contraption.

Their timing was perfect, their placement impeccable. They could be assassins, every one of them.

Evie was the only one out of sync; a feather in their cogs and wheels. How could none of them see that she was broken?

(How had they accepted her so easily into their lives, she was never one of them, she was a wolf in flapper's clothing, just like… just like…)

Where was Livilla?

The show went on, and if the harlequinade was minutes away then it was the saints-and-angel next, the centrepiece of every Saturnalia musette performance. You couldn't put on a show at Saturnalia without the saints-and-angel any more than you could serve wine without water.

This was Livilla's dressing room, and she was not here. What had happened, down in the dark? Was Garnet dead yet? Had Evie failed in her mission?

They couldn't do the saints-and-angel without an angel. Without a stellar.

We're the stellar now, said the light inside Evie's head.

She felt like she was going to throw up. No, not that. She couldn't possibly…

~

TIME LEAPED AHEAD.

Evie stood on stage, lost and vulnerable, singing her lungs out. It was a tragic song, about how angels defend humans without ever really understanding them. Livilla had done it perfectly, every time, every note the same.

It was the stellar, of course, singing through Livilla, just as she now sang through Evie who tasted blood in her mouth as the song was torn from her, every note, every word. She closed her eyes and let the stellar swallow her whole…

She had never once in all her life wanted to be the centre of attention, which was why this was the perfect role for her to play. The saints-and-angel was about reversals, after all.

The story unfolded before the audience. The saint dressed as an angel and the angel dressed as a saint. Sunshine was brilliant, though they faltered when Evie would not meet their eyes in the final scene.

Evie sang and sang and sang, a puppet caught on strings that led to the sky and beyond.

Whatever the stellar was, whatever power it had… How many more of them were there in the sky, waiting to invade?

❧

TIME SPUN and leaped and screeched past the applause, the other songs, the dance, the final bow….

Time stretched forever.

❧

WHEN EVIE CAUGHT up she was in Himself's garret above the box office, and he was yelling at her.

'Wait,' she said, nauseated and giddy. 'I can't…'

He gave her an exhausted look, and kicked a rickety chair in her direction. Evie caught it and sat down, her hands shaking. 'I don't,' she said, and then stopped.

Himself stood over her, light from the lantern reflecting off his spectacles. 'Which one am I talking to now? The killer, or the monster?'

Evie's skin was hot and clammy all over. The creature of light was not gone, it still burned within her, she was sure of it. 'That's an interesting philosophical question,' she started to say.

'You're both smartasses, so that doesn't narrow it down. Are you human?'

'I was this morning.'

He huffed out a breath. 'She stole my show. Quite literally.'

'That was not my idea.'

'You tried to murder Garnet.' His voice cracked on that sentence, as if it mattered more to him than the rest.

Evie's head snapped up. 'Tried?' she said urgently. 'Is he *still* not dead?'

Himself looked pale. 'Livilla said you tried to kill him before the — sky creature dropped her and picked you up. I thought she was lying. Or confused…'

'She prefers to be known as the stellar, not a sky creature,' said Evie, without stopping to think about who had put those words in her head. 'Ugh. I hate that I know that. Do you have anything to drink?'

'I have gin,' said Himself. 'You don't deserve any. *You tried to kill Garnet.*'

'That's my job!' Evie said impatiently. 'It's not personal.'

'It's not —' he laughed hollowly. 'You almost destroyed the world. Do you realise that?'

'Are you speaking to me or the stellar?'

'I don't know which one you are!'

'I'm Evie,' said Evie, feeling slightly offended. 'I'm not the one who goes around with a bunch of different names, Orphan Princel. Stagemaster. Poet. *Himself*.'

He frowned at her. 'What does that last one even mean?'

Oh. Did he not realise all the theatricals called him Himself? That was kind of adorable really.

'I should kill you,' he said, which was a whole lot less adorable.

'Me?' said Evie. 'What did I do?'

'Apart from trick your way into my home and my theatre, pretend to befriend the people closest to me, only to murder the man I —' He broke off then, but what he didn't say spoke volumes.

'If you put it like that,' Evie agreed. 'In my defence, I didn't pretend to make friends, it just sort of… happened.' Sunshine and Christophe and Ruby-red and even Poet and Livilla had taken hold of her heart. She wasn't usually that careless with it. 'What do you mean, I almost destroyed the world?'

Poet sighed at her. 'Who hired you to kill Garnet?'

'I'm not telling you that,' said Evie, offended. 'Dowager Baronnille Augusta Xandelian,' she added a moment later, as the stellar inside her head took over the use of her tongue. 'Damn it. Don't do that,' Evie snapped when she had control back again. 'Why would she even…'

'She's trying to get on my good side,' said Poet dryly. 'She's hoping I'll let her keep you.'

Evie stared at him, horrified. 'How is it up to you?'

'My theatre, my rules. She could have infected one of us when we were fighting the sky, but she chose to come in here, somehow. Hid in the walls, or the beams, or the curtains. If she's a stellar then the only person who has power over her is… the stagemaster.' He said it all so matter-of-factly.

'You can't let her keep my body,' Evie hissed.

'What else are we going to do with it? Can't have you running around trying to kill our Power and Majesty.'

Evie gave him a long look.

'You call yourself the Storyteller, I hear,' Poet said calmly. 'Try this for a bedtime story: if Garnet had died when you put that knife in him, we would have lost the city. We're too weak already, we couldn't take a loss like that. But we — the Creature Court, all the wolves and rats and gattopardi you've met. We defend the earth against the sky, against creatures like that stellar inside your head, and worse. We're the heroes and the soldiers, not the monsters.'

The stellar laughed at that, inside Evie's head, but she did not deny that it was true.

'Tell Augusta Xandelian's son what a hero you are,' Evie said, to see how he would react. After all, the stellar had already revealed the name of her client.

Poet gave her a venomous look. '*He* didn't send you. He knows it doesn't work that way. And I don't know why —' He stopped short. 'Oh, seven hells. He's coming back to the city. That's why his mother wants Garnet dead.'

'I can't tell you anything about my client or her son.'

'Ashiol Xandelian got out of this city alive, he can go fuck himself if he wants more revenge than that.'

Evie had the worst headache, and it was laughing at her inside her skull. 'I don't care,' she said sharply. 'I want you to dig this — stellar out of my head. And then I'll leave the city. I'll leave you alone.'

'I told you that Garnet isn't dead,' said Poet. 'Aren't you honour-bound to finish your assignment, if I free you?'

'I wasn't planning on preventing her,' the stellar said sweetly with Evie's mouth.

'You're not helping,' Evie snapped at her. 'That depends,' she added, glaring at Poet.

'Depends on what?'

'How big of a favour I end up owing you. I don't actually want to leave this city unprotected against an army of stellars. If you really need Garnet alive, then fine, I'll leave him alive. But my professional reputation will take a hit, so you'd better make it worth my while.'

~

THE AUDIENCE HAD GONE HOME. The stage was empty. Evie, still in the bright white angel gown that dripped feathers all over the stage, stood alone.

'I thought you would never go this quietly,' she said to the stellar in her head.

'I got what I came for,' replied the stellar, making Evie's face smile brighter than it ever had before.

'What's that?' It shouldn't bother Evie. It had nothing to do with her. She didn't work for the Creature Court. 'Applause? A pretty white dress? My utter humiliation?'

'I know his weakness now,' said the stellar, and her presence in Evie's head became brighter and brighter. 'Believe me... that's going to be useful.'

Rats ran on to the stage, white rats squeaking and chittering and squeaking. Wolves were there too, two of them, circling Evie, allowing the rats to run over their paws and back. More creatures came. Bats, flapping around in the eaves above. Slender greymoon cats peering from the wings.

Was that a —

Was that a fucking panther?

Weasels skittered past her line of sight and when Evie turned her head... she saw a bear.

A bear.

As Evie recovered from the sight of the menagerie — a literal cabaret of monsters right here on stage, all they needed to do was start singing show-tunes and her surreal dreamscape was complete — the white rats closed in around her feet.

'Time for our curtain call,' said the stellar, like she was enjoying herself thoroughly.

'If I could cut you out of me with a knife, I would,' Evie told her savagely.

The wolves howled. A deep, grinding sound that made Evie's head reverberate with pain. Whiteness blinded her in a searing moment of light, and then...

The rats bit. The wolves snapped. Every creature on the stage came together, snarling and growling, over custody of a white, twitching shape of brightness. The stellar laughed as they tore her apart. The pieces scattered, glowing like fire.

One of Livilla's wolves whimpered, letting a piece of the brightness escape her clamping jaw. The shreds of light grew brighter and brighter, tearing themselves free from the mouths of the creatures.

They came together, every piece of brightness, in the air above the stage, and in the moment before she flew back to the sky she came from, the stellar formed the shape of an angel.

13

SATURNALIA

ONE DAY AFTER THE IDES OF SATURNALIS

*I*t was Livilla, of all people, who gathered up a shaky Evie when it was all over, bundled her in a borrowed coat that smelled of expensive perfume, and walked her on unsteady feet back to the boarding house. Poet and the rest of the Creature Court were nowhere to be seen.

'Why are you helping me?' Evie managed to ask. Her whole body ached like she had been beaten. Her head was scraped raw from the inside out and her throat...

Oh. Her throat was probably sore because of all the singing she had done on stage.

'Didn't you help me?' said Livilla lightly. 'You stole my part, but you also stole the murderous creature that took over my body. On the whole, I came out ahead.'

Evie did not think she would be able to walk without Livilla's sturdy arm around her waist, which was all kinds of embarrassing. 'Is she gone? The stellar.'

'For now,' said Livilla. 'That's never happened before,' she added, in a more subdued voice. 'The sky is something to fight, it doesn't... spy on us, steal our bodies, take an interest in local theatre.'

'She told me,' said Evie, stumbling over her thick tongue. 'She knows his weakness now.'

That disturbed Livilla, though you had to be looking closely to see it, past the thick cosmetic and arch expression. 'It doesn't take a body-swap to see *his* weakness,' she said. 'Anyone could see it from the stars.'

When they reached the boarding house, it was nearly morning. The last shadows of nox bleached out of the sky, ready for a new day.

Evie wasn't sure she could ever look at the sky without fear again. Not now she knew what lived beyond it.

'Keep the coat,' said Livilla, lingering only a moment on the doorstep. 'It will come in useful.'

Evie put her hands in the large, roomy pockets and something crinkled against her hand. She pulled out a clutch of train tickets — four, in all. 'Am I going somewhere?'

'Fast as you can,' said Livilla. 'The war knows your face, now. You can't be here.' She began to walk away, flexing her shoulders in the plain black dress she wore, as if she didn't plan to be human for much longer.

'Won't Garnet be angry you helped me?' Evie called after her.

Livilla turned, a strange look of delight and caution on her face. 'Better me than someone he fears,' she said. 'He'll do less damage that way.'

'You're the reason he's still alive,' Evie remembered. 'You called for help — why do you and Poet follow him, after everything he's done?' She didn't say the name of the Xandelian man, but Livilla must know the violence of which her leader was capable.

'You can't choose your angels,' said Livilla. This time she did walk away. She raised one hand in a careless farewell. 'Stay brilliant, Evie Inglirra.'

'You too,' said Evie quietly, watching Livilla leave.

As she let herself into the boarding house, she was faced with two people: a hulking brute of a man and a quick-eyed, twitchy young boy, carrying a large trunk between them. 'Do I know you?' she asked. She had seen them, she thought, around the theatre, and other places.

Weasels and bears, her mind threw at her.

Neither spoke. They shuffled around her on the landing and left.

Above, there was shrieking, complaining and the sound of suitcases and clothes being thrown back and forth. A single silk stocking fluttered down from the top floor, finally snagging itself on a crack in the bannister.

Evie climbed up and up, until she was slammed against a wall by Sunshine, in a bright silk coat and dark wool hat.

'You're back,' said Sunshine, and kissed her.

Evie allowed herself to be kissed. This, at least, was easy in a morning that had nothing but questions and complications jammed in around her.

'Do you have the tickets?' Sunshine asked, drawing back.

'I do,' said Evie, pulling the crumpled sheaf out of her pocket. 'Are you coming with me?'

'Of course,' said Sunshine. 'I love an adventure.' They winced and pointed up to the attic. The sound of Christophe and Ruby-red screeching at each other could still be heard. 'They're pissed off because Himself sent his boys around to break the news and collect his things. Couldn't say it to our faces, the coward. Either way, he's packing us off.'

Evie looked more closely at the tickets. Orcadia, by way of Etulia. She couldn't say she was sorry to be leaving the country, not with a failed hit behind her, and Garnet likely to be after revenge for the attempt she had made.

'He wants all three of you to come with me?' she managed to say, as she put it all together. 'Is Christophe taking up one of those job offers after all?'

'Perhaps when he stops shouting, he will,' said Sunshine with a twist of their mouth. 'We're theatricals. We always fall on our feet.'

Evie wanted to ask more questions. What message had Himself given them that convinced them leaving the city was an option? What had he told them about Evie herself?

But Sunshine was still looking at her like they were friends, and Evie didn't want to break that any time soon. Besides, they had a lot of packing to do if they were going to be on a train by noon.

'An adventure, you say?' said Evie, and Sunshine glowed in response.

THE AUFLEUR TRAIN station made its usual picture of greys and blacks, of winter coats and tight, tired faces, all wreathed in steam.

The party that Evie travelled with were a little different. Sunshine, Christophe and Ruby-red wore brights and silks like they were about to step on to a stage. Even their luggage was painted in bold shades of teal, forest-green and rose-pink.

Christophe and Ruby-red, once they had recovered from the shock of being dismissed by Himself, and the warning that they must leave the city, settled into the idea that all this was their own grand plan. Christophe waved around a letter of offer from a theatre company in Orcadia, and benevolently promised to get jobs for his friends.

Ruby-red's own ambitions were greater than that: she had read a magazine article about the growing popularity of cabaret in Nova Stella, the city across the wide sea, where they would surely be looking for top class columbines who lived off one meal a day.

Zephyr, it turned out, had disgraced himself by ditching Christophe for a handsome olive merchant's son, which was so unthinkable that everyone had to pretend Christophe had never even thought of ordering an extra ticket in the first place.

The four of them folded easily into the comfortable carriage, well ahead of schedule. Evie couldn't be easy about this journey until they were on their way, but it was still ten minutes to noon, the train boarding slowly around them.

It was Sunshine who saw him coming; Sunshine who nudged Evie and kicked Christophe, pointing down across the platform.

The stagemaster Poet Himself walked out of the swirling steam and smoke, in a dark coat that didn't suit him, like any other passenger.

The theatricals and Evie tumbled out of their carriage like a pile of puppies, throwing themselves at him.

'Are you coming after all?' asked Ruby-red in a haughty voice, and looked gutted when Poet shook his head.

'I came to say goodbye,' he said, and was nearly bowled over by the three of them.

'I hate you,' said Ruby-red, leaving a smacking kiss of red cosmetick on his face.

'Thank you for giving me a chance when you did,' said Sunshine at his other side; they brushed their cheek briefly against his own, and squeezed his hand.

Christophe wrapped his arms fully around Poet's neck and clung like he didn't want to let go, not ever.

'Should have sent you away years ago, Kip,' Poet muttered into his friend's collar. 'You're too bright to be contained in one city.'

'Shut up, you're the worst,' said Christophe, and kissed Poet hard on the mouth. 'Be the stellar,' he said when they came apart. 'For saints sake, give in to how fucking amazing you are. Be the centre of attention for once. But don't play the angel, you look washed out in white. Stick to that Orphan Princel routine of yours, the nobs love you in that.'

'I'll think about it,' said Poet with a small smile. 'Stay brilliant, all of you.'

They waved and crowded back on to the train, leaving Evie and Poet together.

'How can you trust me to look after them?' she blurted out. 'I'm not a theatrical — you know what I am.'

'A monster?' suggested Poet slyly. 'Takes one to know one.'

'I would have thought you'd want me far away from them.'

'Who else is going to protect them?' said Poet, his eyes looking sad and far away behind his spectacles. 'I shouldn't have let myself keep them for so long. Pretending to be — normal, and daylight. When you keep something for yourself, it's a weapon that can be turned against you. I can't afford that. Not now.'

Evie wondered if it was the sky Poet was worried about, or Garnet. 'You love your theatre,' she reminded him.

'I know. I may have to give that up too, but… not yet.'

'So what will you do?' She couldn't talk about the war, the sky, the dangers she had only ever read about in fairy tales. It didn't feel real.

'I'm going to track down those talented children, put my understudies to work. Swap out some of the scripts, bring in a cabaret of monsters. Life is a matinee, my dearling. There's always another show around the corner.'

'I mean, what are you going to do about…' And she glanced up, up at the pale blue-grey sky over the city.

'Oh, that,' said Poet. 'Well. I have a few ideas about that. Don't write me out of the story yet.'

~

EVIE GOT BACK into the carriage, squashing up against Sunshine who had stolen her window seat. Himself stood very still on the platform. As the smoke thickened and the train screamed its departure with one long cry of a whistle, two more figures stepped on to the platform, flanking him.

Evie ducked her head down so she wouldn't be seen as Garnet, on one side of Poet, took his arm. On the other side of him, Livilla leaned a head on his shoulder.

'That demme will be the death of him,' Christophe said bitterly.

'Not the demme,' said Sunshine. 'The bloke, maybe.'

Evie slipped her hand into Sunshine's, and waited for the train to pull out. She half-expected the deadly shape of a gattopardo to break through the window and tear her to shreds in the last moments before they set off, and she didn't drop the thought until the train had passed through three stations.

Even then, she didn't stop holding Sunshine's hand.

'What are you going to do now, Inglirra?' Ruby-red challenged her. 'While we're painting Orcadia's theatre scene scarlet, and showing the world how brilliant we are.'

'Oh,' said Evie. She hadn't been paid for her last job in full and she wouldn't be, now. The newspaper office back home would be angry she had left Aufleur without notice, and she couldn't exactly tell them she was doing it to escape an invisible war that was going to get worse before it got better. 'I guess I'd better do some writing. I get paid by the word, you know.'

Christophe, who still looked somewhat tragic about the day's events, gave her a shaky smile. 'Did you have any particular words in mind?'

'I'm a storyteller,' said Evie. 'I'll think of something.'

THE END

If you enjoyed this novella, Buy the complete Creature Court Trilogy today, starting with Book 1: Power & Majesty.

IMMERSE YOURSELF IN THE GLAMOROUS, DANGEROUS WORLD OF THE CREATURE COURT.

Thanks so much for reading! Please consider leaving a review.

Get a free story when you sign up for my newsletter.

If you enjoyed *Cabaret of Monsters*, you can explore more of the dark and magical world of the Creature Court in this lush, decadent fantasy trilogy full of broken heroes, devastating plot twists and bloodthirsty action:

THE CREATURE COURT

Is Velody ruthless enough to become the next Power and Majesty? Or will the sinister Creature Court destroy everything she loves?

1. Power & Majesty

2. The Shattered City

3. Reign of Beasts

There's also a spoilery epilogue to the series, which you can download for free: Swords of Aufleur.[*]

Visit the Teacup Magic Emporium[†] to get signed paperbacks, bundles, magical merch and bonus content direct from the author!

---

[*] dl.bookfunnel.com/ueqs1yxjym
[†] tansyrr.com/collections/dark-divine

"Clever, witty, and utterly heart-wrenching, this book sparkles
even as it explores real darkness and the terrible consequences of
seeking - or refusing - power."

— STEPHANIE BURGIS ON *POWER & MAJESTY*

ABOUT THE AUTHOR

Tansy Rayner Roberts is an award-winning Australian science fiction and fantasy author who does not make her own gowns, or run across rooftops. She lives with her family in Tasmania and has been known to pick up the occasional embroidery hoop.

Listen to Tansy on Sheep Might Fly, a podcast where she reads aloud her stories as audio serials.

What tea is Tansy drinking? Find out at when you subscribe to her excellent newsletter.*

Follow TansyRR at:
tansyrr.com

Visit the Teacup Magic Emporium† to get signed paperbacks, bundles, magical merch and bonus content direct from the author!

---

* tinyurl.com/tansyrr
† tansyrr.com/collections/dark-divine

DARK & DIVINE TITLES BY
TANSY RAYNER ROBERTS

THE CREATURE COURT

Shapechangers, swords and spice. Stay brilliant!

Power & Majesty

The Shattered City

Reign of Beasts

Cabaret of Monsters

THE RIVER DIVINE

Swords, ravens and sexy assassins

Of Knives & Night-blooms

MYTHIC MAGIC AT THE
EDGE OF THE WORLD

Siren Beat

Join me at the Teacup Magic Emporium* to get signed paperbacks, bundles, magical merch and bonus content direct from the author!

---

* tansyrr.com/collections/dark-divine

GASLAMP FANTASY BY
TANSY RAYNER ROBERTS

SPARKS AND PHILTRES

Faerie Victoriana with Angst & Steampunk

Gate Sinister

House Perilous

Land Glorious

Siege Miraculous

(coming soon)

THE FAMILY CURSEBREAKERS

Vintage cozy fantasy with gargoyles & archaeologists

Curse of Bronze

Tomb of Brass

PRIDE & PREJUDICE RE-
TELLING WITH DRAGONS

A snarky anti-heroine gets her Mr Darcy while protecting her brother
from fortune-hunters

The Season of Dragons

Join me at the Teacup Magic Emporium* to get signed paperbacks,
bundles, magical merch and bonus content direct from the author!

---

* tansyrr.com/collections/dark-divine

OF KNIVES AND NIGHT-BLOOMS

*"Never speak the name of the Black Raven aloud.
Never fail your sacred duty. Never trust magic. And
never travel on the River Divine..."*

CALYX: Didn't mean to bind 3 assassins to her eternal magical servitude, but leaning into it. Has places to be, and a daughter to protect.

IKAROS: Priest of death. Hates this river. Hates boats. Hates that Calyx's magic means he can't kill her. Abandoned by his god. Having a bad week.

DIO: Not even supposed to be here, but kind of into it. Surrounded by hot assassins. Having a great week.

VALERIA: Priest of death. Ageless, deadly, better than all of you. Can kill with a shoe but it probably won't come to that because she is carrying all the knives.

MARDI: Priest of death. Pregnant. Dangerous. Too good for this. One day away from retirement.

REYNARD KALDORAN: Going to kill every last one of you.

THE RIVER DIVINE: Hold my beer.

AN ACTION-PACKED ADVENTURE TALE
OF UNRELIABLE GODS AND BURNT-OUT
ASSASSINS, FROM THE AWARD-WINNING
AUTHOR OF *THE CREATURE COURT*.

Buy "Of Knives & Nightblooms" today.